ESSEX MAN

- A Dave Hunt

by

Steve Bartington

FPP
Fulton Point Publishing

FULTON POINT PUBLISHING

Suite 157

Communications House

9 St John's Street

Colchester

Essex CO2 7NN

www.fultonpoint.co.uk

ISBN 978-1527240292

For Lee Brilleaux, Steve Marriott, and Chris Farlowe. Yes, one of them is still alive, but you know what I mean.

Prologue

Romford Greyhound Stadium, November 1979

A moment ago he'd only his footsteps for company, but now the man who was trudging along the windy tunnel towards the exit heard the steps of someone behind.

He knew what it meant and had suspected it was coming.

He didn't look back, nor did he quicken his pace. His hands were already in the deep pockets of his leather jacket, and he gripped his right hand around the revolver that had been his bedside companion since he had stepped over the line a week or so earlier; the boss liked everyone to remember that he was just that.

He hoped he wouldn't have to use it, and he barely knew how to anyway. He did know, however, that once you drew it, you had no choice. There was no point in trying to scare these people off – they wouldn't work for who they did if there was much chance of that happening. He gripped the cylinder.

Without looking round, he could only guess the distance between him and his tail – forty feet, maybe? It must be twice that far to the exit and the cold dark night, he thought. If he made it, he could live to fight another day.

A large figure in dark clothes emerged at the end of the dimly lit tunnel and put paid to that idea.

"There's someone wants to see you," said the man in black, as he stood blocking any light that might have been at the end of the tunnel.

The man was a giant with fists like hammers, and the man he'd been sent for recognised him from somewhere even though he couldn't put a name to the face. He would have to take his chances with the one behind him. He had a plan.

He stopped dead and waited until the footsteps behind him were close. Then he counted to three, and when he could almost feel the man's breath on his neck, he took out the gun and spun around.

He saw that the man who was tailing him was tall but skinny, almost rake-like – a safer bet than the other one. He raised his arm and brought the butt of the gun down hard against his skull, stunning him and drawing blood. Sensing his chance, he did this three more times, each with more force than the time before. His skinny assailant's face was bathed in blood, yet somehow he stayed upright. One more time, thought the man with the gun and the advantage, and then I can hold this thing to his ribs, and we can make a deal.

But, as he raised his arm for what was surely the last time, he felt something stop it in mid-air, and his arm felt like a twig against the other hoodlum's talon-like grip.

"Be a good boy an' drop it now," said the low voice behind him.

He didn't, even though he was sure he could feel

the bones in his wrist starting to splinter. He hung on for dear life – or at least he did until he felt his arm jerked downwards. Then the pain of his shoulder being wrenched from its socket was too great; the pistol fell to the floor and so did he after an almighty chop landed where his shoulder met his neck.

He was down, and his attempts to crawl were cut short by a hard kick to his rib cage. He collapsed again and fought for breath.

"That'll need stitches," said the man who had delivered the death-chop only a few seconds earlier.

"Yeah, the little *fucker*!" said the smaller man, putting the boot in several times more.

His assailants took a foot each, and the man on the floor never lost consciousness. They dragged him to a nearby car and bundled him into the boot.

Bizarrely, he found himself thinking of Jesus' final journey. Raised a Catholic, he learnt as a boy how Jesus was beaten and lashed so cruelly on the way to his crucifixion that he was almost dead before he got there. He saw a similarity between that and his own situation even though he knew that the Lord Jesus and he lived very different lives.

***

His paymaster sat facing him behind a desk. The room was dark save for a desk lamp, and the boss's outline was silhouetted against a thick haze of cigar smoke. Appropriately, he wore a black suit and tie with a black hat. Combined with the white light of the desk lamp and his ultra-fair skin, it made for an almost colourless scene.

They dragged him to his feet.

"'Allo Bobby," said the man at the top of the table. "I see you've put up a fight," he said, shifting his headlight stare across to the rake-like goon and his bloodied face before bringing it right back to his subject. "I'm glad you learnt something from me: always go down fighting."

He looked up at his two employees once more.

"Anything else to report to me, boys?"

The rake did have something to say, even though the man beside him had tried to convince him not to. "We took this off of him," he said. He drew the pistol from his belt and put it on the desk, as the other goon shook his head in disapproval.

The boss picked up the gun, and all three saw what was coming next.

"I am *very* disappointed in you, Bobby," he said, inspecting the weapon, thumbing the hammer of the old-fashioned pistol. "You always seem to be going off half-cocked.

With that, he pulled the hammer back and blasted four holes in his former employee's chest, as the others did their best not to jump out of their skins. The boss saw that the young man was still breathing, and he circled the desk to where he was now on his knees. Then he wrenched him by the hair, put the barrel at the base of the young man's skull and put eyes in the back of his head.

The men who brought him here watched with disbelief – they thought they were going to rough him up, sling him in a taxi then maybe go for a curry.

Their boss pointed his gun upwards and blew the smoke from the barrel.

"Do you know something?" he said. "Old Clint Eastwood's got nothing on me."

He tossed the gun onto the blood-soaked body, before giving his other employees their orders.

"Whatever plans you had tonight, cancel them. You've got a date with Freddie the foreman – you'd best bung 'im a one for this. Oh, and tidy yourself up," he said to the smaller one. "You look a mess."

Chapter 1

Dave's living room, Colchester, Essex, January 2004

Dave took the record out of the sleeve and laid it on the deck.

There weren't a great number of people with record players left in the early part of the new millennium – fewer still who used them occasionally, and the number of these people in their mid-to-late-twenties was even smaller.

Dave Hunter didn't live entirely in a past that wasn't his own; two years earlier he'd gone out and bought himself a nice modern stereo – a good one too, it had a CD player and everything.

Sadly, a recent fit of rage, egged on by a skipping disc had brought his CD player's life to a violent and premature end, and he joyfully broke it into several pieces and became a vinyl junkie once more (and a happy one, too).

Focusing now, Dave lifted the needle, only to find this wasn't necessary: it sprang to life mechanically along with the turntable. Watching the stylus align itself with the first groove, Dave remembered the excitement of doing this as a young boy every time he saved up enough money for a new AC/DC album. The hum of the turntable's motor and the crackle at the start would build his anticipation. Then one of Angus Young's exhilarating guitar riffs would burst from the speakers, shaking the room and making the world seem like a more colourful and exciting place than he already suspected it really was.

This time, however, there was no guitar riff or any 'bacon crackle' as the needle touched down – or any sound at all. Once again, Dave had forgotten to set his dusty old hi-fi system to 'phono'. A quick flick of the switch and the boy was in business.

"Laaa-deees aaaaand gentlemen. If I could have your attention for a moment please, I would like to

introduce our next act, or should I say … 'artiste'. Now, this boy's come a long way since the days of the sticky mile and the Kursaal, an' 'ee's gonna go a long way further still. Ladies and gentlemen, please make 'im feel at home – Bobby Fulton and his band!!!"

A brief crowd cheer soon hushed and gave way to a loud and overdriven guitar riff. Despite its grainy texture, Dave instantly recognised it as the intro to *The Price Of Love*. Not really standard fare for a blues band, although their vocalist (who Dave presumed was Mr Fulton) did lend it a certain pub-rock authenticity. With a vocal style similar to that of the late, great Lee Brilleaux, this version contained a menace not heard in the Everly Brothers' classic original.

Dave listened to the track attentively, unable to decide whether he liked it or not. He was a huge blues fan and also a bit of a purist when it came to what had once been described as 'the devil's music'. This contained all the right ingredients – bottleneck guitar, wailing harmonica, a whiskey-soaked singing voice – but Dave felt it was a bit too close to the pub-rock territory of bands like Ducks Deluxe or Eddie and the Hot Rods.

A few bars into the next song, a nerve-jangling take on Willie Dixon's *Diddy Wah Diddy*, Dave felt himself warming to the band and their blokey, blustery, high-octane take on his favourite genre. So there was an element of pub-rock about them – so what? It was this snobbery that had, many years ago, nearly made him dismiss fellow Essex bluesmen Dr Feelgood – and where would he be without them now, eh? The thought of it!

Also, he imagined these musicians were cut from similar cloth to him – something else he found endearing about them. He knew from the MC's announcement that they were from the same area as him, but judging by the sound, this was a band that had walked the boards of the same circuit that he had (and by the sound of it, had got something in return, too).

Turning the volume down, he sat back on his couch and lit a cigarette; he wasn't in the mood for loud music.

Just something to scare away the eerie silence.

It was a Sunday afternoon in January, the worst day of the week in the worst month of the year, and Dave had the place to himself – in fact, he lived by himself.

He looked at his living room clock: 4:15 pm. He looked out his window and saw that darkness was falling rapidly. A murky cloud cover drifted in, and the sun sank as if for the last time. Similarly, Dave's mind began to drift.

He thought of how, in just under four months, he would finish the second year of his music degree, leaving him with nothing to do for three months. *Three months!* His heart, mind and lungs filled with thick, black dread at the thought of having no true purpose for this length of time.

He tried to think of ways he could pass the time, but this only made him feel worse. He could do some voluntary work, perhaps, or maybe take a drive down to Canvey to seek out some old 'Feelgood' haunts, if any were still standing. This would take up an afternoon at best if he did it slowly. And what was the point? What could this possibly achieve?

Nothing, that's what.

Doubtless, there would be memorabilia on display. A few signed pictures, maybe, or some posters with faded faces, the usual, but Dave knew this was meaningless. In the face of mind-numbing emptiness, recreational activities offered feeble resistance.

In need of something else to think about, Dave turned his attention once more to the disc now spinning silently on his turntable and wondered why he found himself listening to a record that had been in his collection for what could be described as quite some time (almost two-and-a-half-years). Not only was he confused as to why he had put it off for so long, but he did not know why he had chosen today to give it a spin. Was he bored?

One thing he did know was that he'd not given it a moment's thought in all the time he had had it.

The record had turned up outside a Salvation Army shop that was now a bookmakers, and he had bought it almost certain that he would never play it (something all music lovers do from time to time). As it did then, the lightly faded LP cover showed a man in a denim shirt, teeth bared and chest on display, playing a mean-looking harmonica underneath what looked like a very hot, very bright stage light. It was in black and white too, lending the picture some grainy retro authenticity.

This hadn't been enough to make Dave play it, of course. In fact, shamefully, he could remember thinking something at the time along the lines of 'oh no, how depressing, another forgotten white-boy-British-blues-wannabe' (despite being almost this himself), as well as something along the lines of 'can't they just let it go?'

If he had thought he was smart dismissing them in this way then, he felt stupid for it now. He wanted to know more. In fact, he wanted to know a lot more.

Chapter 2

About 39 miles away, in the communal area of a shared flat, high up in a tall council housing cabinet, a tall, tattooed man skulked fearsomely. He was a delightful soul, and he went by the name of –

Slouch (57)

The man known as Slouch claimed he was given this name because he most definitely wasn't one, which seemed believable enough. However, it was hard not to notice that his shoulders hung (slouched?) in a manner that suggested his ancestors may have missed one or more key stages in the evolutionary process.

Slouch was a big man, who liked to look intimidating, always liked to look hard. Even when he wasn't hanging out with his unsavoury colleagues or terrorising night-time petrol station attendants.

His ability to exude menace had got him where he was today. That, and a reputation for being a bit of a psycho was everything the would-be hoodlum needed to get started, to get 'in' with the big boys, and Slouch had thirty years of gainful employment behind him to prove it.

He was heavily tattooed, this Slouch fellow. He'd had more pricks than University Challenge and more stains than a whore's mattress, and he liked to think the latter enhanced his scary demeanour. Recently, he had started to suspect that his ability to scare people off was better than actually hitting them – he was getting too old for all that. Not that there was anything wrong with a spot of mindless violence now and again – far from it, in fact – but Slouch had wondered in recent years if he was quite the wrecking ball he used to be. He knew security staff were forbidden from carrying firearms in this country, but what if, just what if, one day an especially brave night watchman did have the balls to front him out while number two radioed for backup?

He could be jumped left, right and centre by a half-dozen of 'em. And while he was fairly sure he could still punch, kick, gouge and butt his way out of a situation like this, he wasn't completely sure of it.

As a younger thug, this had never been a problem. Back then, banks could have used Indian tigers to patrol their grounds and keep an eye on their safes and Slouch would have been able to stand his ground (and probably wrestle one to it), such was his presence.

It was his bulky, towering presence that, following his dismissal from the army for being too dangerous, had made Slouch one of the most sought-after heavies going, and the offers of work soon came flooding in. And although he'd had no intention of leaving Essex, he was flattered to have been approached to work for a leading city firm.

Slouch didn't know much about the criminal

underworld's infrastructure, back then, but he knew that working for a London firm was about as good as it got, and he had entertained the idea. But not for long.

Slouch wasn't fussy whose fingers he broke, but he was fussy about where he went to do it. Canvey, Southend, Baaahsildon – that little neck of the woods. That was where 'e belonged. Slouch was a home counties boy at heart, and he wasn't interested in anything the city had to offer.

But on this damp and dreary Sunday evening, in this damp and dreary council flat, Slouch found himself wondering if he had truly done the right thing.

He didn't know powerful forces had plans for him, but they did, and he would soon be thrust into action one last time. He planned his retirement as people his age did, but not many of them would get the kind of leaving party he was about to.

Chapter 3

The pub. On a night like this there was nothing else for it, and as Dave finished scraping away the last cold, sad remnants of his TV dinner, he knew he was on his way.

This lifted his spirit in a way that other less civilised sections of society (non-pub-goers, teetotalers, etc.) simply wouldn't understand.

Dave, you see, loves *the pub.*

And whenever Dave talked quite openly about his love of *the pub,* he would explain that he means he loves *the pub as in the great institution that is the British public house.* However, he usually went on to explain that he also loves *the pub as in his local, The Red Lion,* too.

His detractors could argue that he was preaching to the converted here since Dave only ever gave these talks *in* the pub (as in the great institution, although more often than not it was in The Red Lion, too), but he did it anyway. After all, it was well-intentioned and more enjoyable and less offensive than some of the stuff you heard there.

Plus, anybody on speaking terms with Dave Hunter knew that having any kind of argument with him was a pointless and dispiriting exercise. Trying to make him consider an angle that was in any way different to his own was like cornering a Dalek and trying to convince it that violence and aggression were bad and that maybe, just maybe, there is a good soul in there who just hasn't been loved enough.

In short, it was impossible, and if somebody became impatient with him during one of these lively debates and swung for him (a surprisingly rare occurrence), it pleased him no end. Why? Because in his mind this proved that he was right. "You see!" he'd once said while cupping a bloody nose with his right hand and doing some serious finger-wagging with his left one. "I was right all along!"

There would be none of this nonsense tonight, though. A nice relaxing evening was what Dave wanted. A few drinks, some utterly pointless conversation with the locals, maybe put a few quid in the jukebox – he struggled to see how anyone could ask for more.

As he put his faded Levi's jacket on and looked around for his boots, he wondered who would be in. This was what made going down the local so special. You never knew what to expect, but even if nothing special happened you would still have a good time.

Before leaving the house, Dave took a moment to spare a thought for all the poor souls watching *Antiques Roadshow* this evening.

Even church wasn't as bad as that.

About half an hour after Slouch entered the grotty little council flat inhabited by some of the county's finest prostitutes (and entered one of them, too), he closed the door behind him and made his way to the lift. It was the same Slouch that had walked down the same corridor thirty-five minutes ago, although his slack-jawed grin and the spring in his step made him seem like a different man entirely to the miserable old sod he'd been when he got there.

The lift arrived after a two-minute wait, a period of time that on a normal day might have had the power to annoy him. Not today though, or not now, anyway. He got in the lift £25 poorer but emotionally and spiritually a good deal richer.

What is it about these Asian birds, Slouch wondered as the lift descended – drove him nuts, they did. It was during his spell in the army that he'd discovered his love of paying for sex with women from around the globe, and it was a passion that he held to this day. His stationing in 1960s Germany had given a young Slouch the opportunity to sample the country's glorious, notorious Reeperbahn, although he soon realised that, as with Amsterdam's De Wallen (the red-light district), this was just something the tourists did. And, horror of horrors, he also learnt that backpacking British mummy's boys (i.e. students – always Slouch's least favourite people) did the same thing, often as a rite of passage. He wasn't having that, so he ventured south to the city of Bonn, whose culture he fell in love with immediately (especially the *Verrichtungsbox,* which was basically a sex drive-in).

He'd enjoyed these smash 'n' grab raids so much that he almost forgave the bastards for trying to kill his old man twenty years earlier – almost.

But not quite.

Time went by, and further overseas postings took him to America, where he found Puerto Rican hookers in New York who were dirtier than the sidewalks they walked along at night. They were more used to entertaining wimpy Wall Street types, but Slouch soon found that they were just as good with *'real big men like you like soldier or sailor boy'*, as one of them had called him.

Slouch loved all this variety, but the best was yet to come, and he soon discovered that the crème de la crème, the high priestess of 'bang-for-your-buck' (or 'pay-per-do!'), was the Chinese girl. And he hadn't had to go to China and eat cat and dog to find out, either.

Casual racism was standard fare in the circles that Slouch moved in, as was a mostly negative attitude towards migrant workers. Slouch went along with this, but his heart was never really in it, for he had no problem with the illegal influx into the area – especially not the womenfolk forced to make a modest living from the world's oldest profession. They may have taken work from the local girls (many of whom he knew), but to Slouch it was a buyer's market as well as a service industry.

His warm recollections were interrupted by a ping that told him the lift had reached the ground floor.

He walked past half a dozen overfilled wheelie bins to his BMW and handed a fiver over to one of the two young boys he had asked to 'wotch 'is motah', even though Slouch knew it was an honour for a boy to guard a man's car.

Slouch felt a second's genuine sadness at the sight of these street kids who were too young to be out after dark, before reminding himself that many years ago it would have been him out on that same quiet corner. He'd turned out alright, hadn't he?

Feeling in need of a little lift (he was knocking on a bit) he hit play on his car stereo once he was moving. It was Status Quo's latest CD, entitled *Heavy Traffic*. He hadn't liked their last few albums, but this one featured a song called *The Oriental*.

And Slouch *loved* that.

Chapter 4

Dave stepped out of the rain into the welcome warmth of the tap-room smog, wondering what fancy new name the smoking room would be given if certain people ever got their way.

The pub was busy for a Sunday night, and it was the usual mix of hooded tops, muddy boots and used-car salesman that you got in a home counties hostelry. They got along, mostly. And when they didn't? Well, the injuries were fairly minor.

Having decided to keep his jacket on in spite of the roaring log fire, Dave walked up to the bar and ordered a pint with a whisky chaser. As always when he was drinking alone, he amused himself by eavesdropping on other people's conversations. On one side he heard a chap in a West Ham top explaining that "bein' in the *Premiership* is all abaaht *consistency*," while a friend listened intently. On the other, he heard someone describing a recent fight in which he had seemingly been the victor. Dave considered the very strong possibility that his opponent was in a different pub, right now, telling the very same story. Then, Dave tuned into a conversation over by the pool table and heard another boastful tale, only this chap was more lover than a fighter, and Dave decided he didn't want to hear this.

Drinking it all in, he reflected that, in the case of the menfolk at least, the three R's once so beloved of his country's education system had been replaced with three *F's*. Yes, he thought, modern man was obsessed with football, fighting and *fumbling*.

And why not, he thought – it's better than talking about the weather.

"How'd you get on last night in the end?" asked Dennis, the pub's cheery landlord, as he handed Dave his change and broke his train of thought.

"Last night?"

"Yeah, last night. You were talking about some kind of 'professional engagement' involving this band of yours. A 'jig' or something I believe you call it?"

Ah yes, thought Dave, the gig. He must mean last night's 'jig' in a freezing cold barn somewhere in Norfolk, in a setting so rural that he'd feared the worst when he'd asked where the mains were.

"Not too bad actually," Dave replied, only half lying since it had been none too clever either. "Bit of a slow start, reasonable turnout, bit rusty after the Christmas break."

"Could have been worse, then?" said Dennis. "I mean if you were *really* unlucky, one of the local farmers could have offered you his daughter's webbed hand in marriage. *HA HA HA!*" Nobody found the joke quite as funny as the man who told it, but it did elicit some sniggering from a pair of farm workers who, like Dave, were busy making sure the bar didn't fall over. Sensing an audience, Dennis turned to the two tractor boys for the follow-up:

"'Ere, what do you call the sweat on your bollocks when you're screwing your cousin?" Dave sighed and silently mouthed the words 'relative humidity' as Dennis said it loud enough for two. Dennis followed it with his trademark '*HA HA*' but stopped short of the final '*HA!*' when he realised he'd pushed it too far (and lost his audience). He shook his head, murmured something unpleasant, and went back to polishing glasses.

In spite of his lousy sense of humour, Dennis was a decent chap and popular with the locals, including Dave. Like many in the licensed trade, Dennis wore a shirt and tie while he was serving (although green-on-light-green was an unusual colour combo, it had to be said). Also like many in the licensed trade, he was of indeterminate age; he looked about forty and probably always had done as did almost every publican in the land. Dennis had certainly looked this old when he'd bought The Red Lion fourteen years ago with his wife, Glenda, who was nice enough but who was rarely seen these days for some reason or another. Dennis hosted the occasional lock-in but only when he felt his customers needed it and not just whenever they wanted one.

Yes, Dennis was a good man, and Dave liked him.

Dave also liked his pub The Red Lion, even if there was one thing wrong with it: you had a better chance of having a drink with Muddy Waters than you did of enjoying a pint of Dave's beloved Estuary Lager.

Estuary Lager was brewed by The Estuary Ale Company, a micro-brewery and sister company of the better known Kentish Ale Company. Their lager was not dissimilar to Carlsberg (which tonight would have to do), only made with softer water, a finer finish and a more sophisticated palette in mind. It was also stronger – a man's lager in Dave's opinion.

Sadly, recent times had seen a dip in the company's fortunes, perhaps a lasting effect of 90s 'lad culture' and its endorsement of the more mainstream Stella Artois and Budweiser. Estuary Ale was surviving, but only just (in spite of Dave's best efforts to make them thrive once more).

Dave wandered over to the jukebox and started thumbing through the selections. Although this one didn't play the superior vinyl like the beautiful Wurlitzer machines of old, it did at least contain discs – albeit of the compact variety. Any blues, he wondered. No? Okay, that's to be expected, these people are philistines after all. What else have we got, then?

He eventually settled on a 60s soul compilation and punched in some choice cuts. Otis Redding. Wilson Pickett. Ray Charles. The real stuff – far more intoxicating than the liquor in his cup (although, to be fair, they did complement each other fabulously).

His next stop was the pool table, where he wiped the floor with the boasting lothario he'd overheard earlier in two best-of-threes. He'd done the usual thing, walked over and feigned a nervous interest which earned him an invitation to play. The bloody fools!

Declining an offer of switching to darts (at which he was equally skilled), Dave Hunter bid farewell to his new friends with his usual 'good to meet you, good to beat you' and made his way back to the bar. On his way there he visited the jukebox again to see if The Faces' *Pool Hall Richard* was available. It wasn't.

Almost the second that Dave put his empty glass down he heard Dennis bellowing "Last orders … PuuuuhLEASE!" in a manner suggesting he'd been to RADA in another life and not the Falklands as he sometimes claimed.

"One for the road is it, sir?"

33

Dave knew he had lectures in the morning, and with that in mind, he decided that he definitely did want another drink. Fucking lectures. Uni-fucking-versity. More time in that pseudo-intellectual bath-house grief-hole that would be his home for the next eighteen months.

"Dennis," he said, "make it a double."

Sunday bloody Sunday.

Chapter 5

YR 2 STUDENTS' NOTICE

FOR PERSONAL REASONS, PROF. ROLPHS SHALL

NOT BE ATTENDING LECTURES THIS MORNING.

ALL CLASSES TO BE RESCHEDULED AT THE

EARLIEST CONVENIENCE.

So read the sign outside CA3, the place of so many highlights of Dave's academic career.

"This is, out*RAGEOUS*!" declared one rather militant young woman (others were lending some thought as to what these personal reasons might be, and just how personal they were). "People have spent their *OWN MONEY* to get here ..." (Mum and Dad's money, probably love, Dave thought, correcting her mentally, but definitely *not* verbally.) "And now we're just being *SENT AWAY*, with barely a *WORD* of an expla*NATION*. It's just not *ON!*"

A few of the other dozen or so students nodded loosely in agreement with the young woman whose voice went up at the end of phrases like an Australian soap actor, but Dave couldn't help wondering if they felt forced into doing so.

He'd found out the hard way that it was best not to disagree with somebody who stood for free speech (and wore badly plaited hair, and was an active member of the Students' Union, etc., etc.) and he was sure that others had learned from this. Much easier just to feign casual agreement, he noted sourly.

Dave had never said anything offensive to Miss Aura Adcock. All he said was … It doesn't matter what he said. Let's just say he wouldn't be on her Christmas card list this year and probably not next year either. If she still sent cards and celebrated the festive season, which she probably didn't for one reason or another.

Truth be told, Dave wasn't bothered about the lecture. He had a headache, and he felt queasy after last night's bender, and his heart just wouldn't have been in it.

He ambled along to the café that overlooked the campus square, with its huge open-air chessboard and the giant welded parrot, and he saw the table that was occupied by two of his friends and one other chap. The first one of his friends that he saw at the table was a young man by the name of –

Daniel Blyth, 20

A would-be concert pianist – would-be in as much as the family piano teacher, unbeknownst to his wealthy parents, had introduced Danny to Little Richard, Fats Domino and the only 'professor' Danny had any real respect for. Danny made no bones about the fact that he knew his claret from his beaujolais, and he was from the kind of family where this was expected.

Speaking of booze, Daniel Blyth liked it a lot, and he liked lots of it, too. He was reckless and irresponsible, and Dave found both of these traits appealing and endearing.

He was a skinny 6'1" and he had chin-length black hair which earned him occasional piss-takes in the working-class boozers he had been unaccustomed to visiting before university, oddly enough. Danny had a vicious wit, though, and despite his androgyny, he had a stinging left hook, and anybody who mocked him usually only did it once.

He actually put Dave in mind of the late Rolling Stone Brian Jones, the posh boy turned R&B brawler; the kid from a good home who was so easily corrupted by his friends 'Mick 'n' Keef'.

Danny was always happiest at the start of a new term, unlike most students who couldn't wait to get blotted before the ink had dried on their final test papers. The reason? Well, at the end of term, Danny had to return to the home of the Blyth family – actually a sprawling country estate in rural Surrey – of which he was very much the black sheep.

Here, he learnt of his brother's excellence, as his father sung (or slurred, depending on the time of day) the deepest praise of Miles Blyth Jr., Danny's elder brother and a military man just back from a tour of Iraq. Worse, his younger sister Violet, a naughty little slip of a thing, had recently started working in the city and was now taking steps towards being a responsible, respectable adult (that's what Daddy thought, anyway!)

Danny couldn't compete with this, and he didn't even try. His family didn't appreciate him, but his friends did.

Yes, Danny was a top bloke, thought Dave, as was –

Mick Davies, 19

Seemingly the sensible one of the trio (and the three of
them did perform together), Mick was something of an 'I'
to Danny's 'Withnail'. That's not to say he didn't have his
moments, but he did have a responsible nature perhaps on
account of his background. For where a certain Daniel
Peter Blyth knew his claret from beaujolais, little Mickey
Davies was more accustomed to chalking darts and finding
fifty-pence pieces for the electric meter.

Where Danny was tall, Mick was wide. In another
life, he could have been a rugby player, if only he'd been
born with a plummy accent and a less proletarian name. His
musician's fear of an early rise didn't help, of course (if a
guitarist isn't playing on a Saturday night, then you can just

bet he's drinking).

Danny favoured pricey, bohemian attire, but Mick's get-up was distinctly blue-collar (and composed largely of blue denim, too). He also liked long-sleeved checked shirts, which he rarely bothered tucking into his jeans.

Musically, he was a deceptively gifted guitarist. He favoured hollow-body electrics and, unlike many so-called blues guitarists, he was capable of throwing some T-Bone Walker and some Charlie Christian into the mix (something you didn't hear much when white boys tried to play the blues). Barre chords and whole-tone bends were meat and drink to him, and he had developed the necessary left-hand strength to master these techniques with the help of his old guitar teacher, who had told a fourteen-year-old Mick to switch to masturbating with his other hand.

Mick Davies also had, at great personal effort, recently mastered charts (or 'dots' as they were sometimes called in an attempt to sound clever by people who actually weren't). Therefore, Mick was as adept at classical guitar (which he loved dearly) as he was at blues and anything else that he was asked to play. He was an awesome slide player too – the kid was going places.

Mick was also, unbeknownst to him, the inspiration behind a song Dave was working on called *Last of the Denim Cowboys*. The song was some way from complete, but Dave had the key, the groove and the greasy rock 'n' roll/rhythm 'n' blues feel that a song like this needed all in place. And boy, did he have a killer set of opening lines:

Well, he comes from a factory town,

Somewhere in the Dirty South.

He was born too late, maybe '78,

With a greasy spoon in his mouth ...

Dave knew you couldn't rush these things, but that didn't stop him champing at the bit to show the song to his bandmates, and then later to tell his unassuming guitarist that he was, in fact, the story's hero and protagonist.

That is if he couldn't pitch the song to his hero Steve Gibbons first, the man for whom this blue-collar tale set to a Chuck Berry rhythm was surely written if not the greatest song that Gibbons never wrote.

The third person at the table was a smooth-talking American exchange student with a silly name. Dave had disliked him from the moment he'd met him, and while campus etiquette seemed to suggest that he ought to keep this to himself, some people had picked up on it anyway.

Cooley Ritter, 22

It wasn't just his slimy disingenuousness that Dave loathed about American exchange student Cooley Ritter, but this didn't help things, either. It wasn't that his parents had followed the strange American tradition of putting a surname where his Christian name should be, and nor was it his constant pining for his 'gal' back home, one Ms Vegas Sky (even Dave admitted that was pretty cool).

It all boiled down to one thing. Or at least, one person. One female person.

Ah, yes. The girl.

Dave remembered and probably always would remember the first time he saw this lovely young lady, one fateful day the September before last. It must have been love, as she was wearing a Rolling Stones lips logo t-shirt and had a saxophone carry-satchel over her left shoulder with a book entitled *Soul to Swing* hanging out: this was before he heard her play the damn thing (think Bobby Keys, only much better looking). Then he noticed her hair, which was chestnut-brown like her eyes, and which he imagined catching the light of the sun on a bright, fine day.

There was more. She had a naughty giggle with a bit of a hiss, and she slapped her hand over her mouth as she did this. In a charming, tomboyish touch she wore an LA Lakers jacket, and dark blue jeans that hugged madly at her hips 'n' ass. Dave had it, and he had it bad.

Whether or not she was enamoured with his Snail's Pace Slim hairstyle, receding at the front, long and ponytailed at the back, his twenty-a-day habit and his craggy outdoors exterior in this distinctly metrosexual environment was as yet to be seen.

Mr Ritter was showing interest too, and while Dave hated to admit it, his nemesis did seem to have taken the lead.

If news ever got back to him that Mr Ritter had 'touched down' with her or whatever the Yanks called it (and it would get back to him in a place like this), Dave swore that he would take revenge. He might not kill him, but he would certainly say that he had seen him touch one of the children from their work experience programme.

All Dave knew was that although the Yank was in the lead, if ever he got in 'pole position' with her, he'd be taken down quickly but not without suffering first.

"David!" exclaimed Danny getting to his feet as Dave got to the usual table, back-row, by the window. "Ya' look a bit flimsy, old boy. Have you … Have you been drinking?" asked Danny with mock horror.

"Guilty, yer 'onour," said Dave as he sat himself down.

"I see. A full confession – how very noble of you," said Danny using sarcasm at just the right time. "Anything else before we begin sentencing?"

"No," said Dave, hanging his head as he did so, "I know I've done wrong, and I know I deserve what's coming to me. I can even suggest a punishment – I think I should be sent back to bed for twenty-four hours with nothing more than a tub of Mars Ice Cream and a Playboy bunny for company, should I feel up to it later."

"You'll be lucky," said Mick, returning from the self-service counter. "You'll have to make do with this," he said, as he handed Dave a cup of the finest fair-trade coffee in town.

"And the Playboy bunny?"

Silence fell as Mick sat down and the hangover/courtroom charade was over. As usual, Danny piped up and broke the silence.

"So, what do we reckon old Rolphy's been up to then, eh? The old slag."

"I reckon he's had an affair – or a breakdown," was Dave's preliminary verdict. "I mean come on, we've met his wife, and we've seen what she's like. Hey, if I was married to that, I'd try both those things." He sipped his coffee. "Or just play it safe and fake my own death."

They had indeed met Hilary Ralphs once before.

47

Then, they had been frozen still by her icy stare, and now, over a year later, each of them shivered at the memory.

"I bet she wears the trousers indoors," Mick came in with. "Ironically enough."

There was a pause.

"Ironic how?" asked Danny.
"Well, he always 'jokes' about her spending all their money on clothes, caning it on dresses she never wears."

"Hey, maybe she caught him wearing them, and she's gone back to her mum's – his stories do sound like a cry for help sometimes," said Dave, getting a laugh from two of the three.

He turned to the unimpressed-looking man he disliked so strongly. "What about you then, *Abraham Lincoln.* What do you reckon's upset the Prof so much that he's prepared to miss hearing his own voice for once?"

"I don't know … Maybe he found a spider in the

bathtub or something," said Ritter in the nasal 'Noo Yoarrk' accent which Dave hated but a certain girl seemed to like, unfortunately. "Look, the professor is clearly going through a difficult time here, okay? We should respect his privacy and his dignity."

"I see," said Dave.

That was that, then.

Dave felt ashamed once the laughter had died down. The Prof was alright, and in fact, Dave felt quite sorry for him. Professor Rolphs was an intellectual heavyweight, but he was otherwise small and insignificant.

And he knew it, poor sod.

It had saddened Dave to see this, for although he knew that many 'uni-types' found *him* amusing, with his swaggering walk and his fighter's stance and his boxer's nose, at least he knew that if it was necessary, he could survive in the wild and they wouldn't.

"Well, I guess it's too early for the pub," said Dave,

surprising everybody including himself. "But we're all

packing, right? Whaddayasay we go blow up some dust?"

Chapter 6

A long, long way from all this (Basildon, to be precise), a man was sitting at a table in a roadside café, trying not to flick cigarette ash on the tablecloth. It was fair to say that his reputation preceded him.

'Left-Handed' Pete, 58

A bit of a throwback, with his once-black, slicked-back pompadour (now distinctly silvery) and goatee beard, yellowed by a twenty-a-day habit, 'Left-Handed' Pete wore the sleeves of his white button-up way past his elbows like painter-decorators did back in the day, and had tucked his shirt into faded baby-blue drainpipe jeans. Unsurprisingly, his get-up was rounded off with a thick-set pair of jet-black, leopard-skin and pattern-tongued 'brothel creepers' which were impractical for dancing to rock 'n' roll in, but handy in other circumstances, he'd found over the years.

With nicotine-stained fingers, he stirred his tea over a Peter Stuyvesant (he was in one the last cafés around that still let you do this); again, taking care not to get ash on the red-and-white-checkered PVC which these places always seemed to lay their tables with. He knew Slouch would be late – he always was – and it wasn't a problem.

Lateness was only a problem on a job, where seconds counted, and timing was everything. Then it was a big problem.

Pete looked around and drank the atmosphere in. He liked these little cafes you found by the side of the road; he reckoned they had character. Not like these poncey little chain places that had sprung up everywhere while he wasn't looking. He hated them and refused to go in them.

He put two sugars in his tea and wondered what his doctor would say about this – probably the same thing he'd say about the fag in one hand and the gold-label milk he stirred in with the other (he was known as 'Left-Handed'

52

Pete, but he was, in fact, ambidextrous). Fortunately for the doc and himself, he kept his café breakfasts down to one a week. He and Slouch had been meeting for breakfast on a Monday morning for many years, and it was a tradition he intended to keep up. They had earned it too, working the doors at weekends, dealing with all the rabble.

This weekend had been particularly nasty out there on the frontline, for one reason or another. Pure carnage – might have something to do with the cheap cocaine the boss was selling. Pete had asked to be kept out of all that – 'orrible, nasty stuff.

At the same time as the clock above the entrance told him it was 10:15, Pete saw his friend's 'beamer' coming into the mud-and-gravel car park out front. He took a look at the menu.

Slouch liked this café as well, not for their relaxed attitude to the smoking ban (he'd packed that up years ago) but because he could bring Rambo, his large Alsatian in with him. It didn't seem right leaving the poor thing home all alone while he lived it up, and it wasn't like anyone was going to complain now, was it?

Pete put his newspaper down, as Slouch took his seat and Rambo settled down under the table.

"Hope you're 'ungry," said Pete, the first one to speak as usual.

After studying the menu for a minute or two, Pete raised a finger and caught the eye of the establishment's deathly overweight proprietor, Barry. Barry wobbled over with a pen and paper and a small plate of scraps for Rambo. On the house, natch.

"What'll it be then, fellas?" he asked cheerfully, despite being short of breath from the walk over.

As usual, 'Left-Handed' Pete did the talking.

"We'll have a nice 'elfy Full English Feast for my friend 'ere," he began in his slow Cockney drawl, "and beans on toast for me'self – I'm watching me figgah!" he said when he saw that his slimmed-down order had earned him a funny look from his friend. Baz scribbled this down and began the long journey back to the counter.

"Here you go, boy," said Slouch, as he put the plate of bacon rinds under the table for his beloved dog.

As he sat back up, his friend made eye contact.

"So, you got the message then?"

"Yeah," said Slouch with a little nod. "I got the message."

That morning, both men and several others in the organisation had received a burn-after-reading-style letter from the boss, telling them to meet him at his Southend-on-Sea golf lodge clubhouse on Friday. At 4:00 am.

It was unlike their boss to contact his employees directly; he'd moved with the times, and his organisation had layers of management like any other slick, modern corporation. No, this was a rallying of the troops, and both men knew it.

"Sounds dodgy, if you ask me," said Slouch quietly.

"Well, Slouch, I don't think he's looking for volunteers to help out at his local church fete, now is he?"

His friend didn't need to answer.

"We're gettin' too old for this," said Slouch with a note of sadness in his voice.

"You're telling me, mate," Pete replied. "I'm nearly sixty, for heaven's sake. I'm retiring next year, and while I like the idea of retiring to a B and B on the Isle of Wight, I don't want it to be the one 'er Majesty has shares in, Gawd bless 'er."

This blessing of the Queen was sincere, for although 'Left-Handed' Pete had spent many of his fifty-eight years abusing the laws of her land, he still had great admiration for 'the old gal' as he called her.

"I don't like this, don't like it at all," said Slouch, shaking his head as he did so. "Either someone's gonna get hurt, or something's gonna get stolen." He took a sugar sachet from the bowl on the table and shook it a bit. "Or both," he said, looking up at his mate.

"Or worse," said Pete, looking Slouch right in the eye.

"No – we don't do that."

"If you say so, mate. If you say so."

The trouble with working for the kind of organisation they did was that it was a contract you could never, ever break.

On the surface, there was omerta in the criminal community, an implied brotherly bond that ran deeper than blood ties if necessary. But in truth, this was sentimental bullshit and little more than a control mechanism. There was no honour among thieves, none whatsoever, and when someone high up said jump, you jumped.

And when he tells you to take a fall, well, you did that too. It was the Freemasons. It was the Hotel California. You could never leave.

The younger ones, which was what Slouch and 'Left-Handed' Pete had once been, were keen to get a break, eager to show their commitment to the cause and to show that they were up there with the big boys. What they didn't realise was that by doing this they were actually selling something priceless: their souls. They found that out later – too late, usually – and although they were paid well for this transaction, it could never be enough. Not for that.

Soon, a fat wobbling man would bring them their breakfast. Neither of them felt very hungry.

Chapter 7

Around noon, a tall, greyish-haired man took his first step of the day outside, into his vast acres of garden. He lit a large, expensive cigar with a small, expensive lighter, sucking on the end for a moment as the taste and the smell worked their magic. It had been a difficult morning.

His wife had gone out earlier, probably off on her weekly tanning expedition, which had freed him up for a few hours. Normally, he'd use this time for leisurely pursuits – a round of golf or a quick swim, perhaps, maybe have lunch at the club etc.

Today, however, the boss had spent the morning planning. What he was working on was illegal, immoral and highly dangerous (and if properly executed, likely to make him a fortune on top of the one he already had, too).

It had its risks, for sure, but this was a man who loved taking risks and enjoyed a challenge. His name was the one that everybody knew:

Norman Layer, 59

Without question one of the wealthiest, most powerful –
and most feared – men in Essex and London, the garden he
was standing in now was so big that he could have played
cricket there and not had to worry about his neighbour's
greenhouse if somebody hit a six. If he was prepared to
scuff the lawn that was tended by his team of gardeners,
that was. Which he wasn't.

He owned a fleet of vintage cars, and he had a
private garage on the side of his house where they were all
kept in running order. He even had someone working on
getting him the 1963 Aston Martin driven by Sean Connery
in the film Goldfinger. He was going to get it no matter
what, and he didn't care whether somebody stole it for him
or if he had to pay the asking price – neither was beyond

his means.

He owned a golfing lodge, eight nightclubs, four restaurants, God knows how many pubs and even more houses.

In many ways, he was the perfect host. Guests in his nightclubs (four in Southend, two in Basildon, one in Brentwood and one in Romford) were treated to a supply of, if not the finest, then certainly the cheapest cocaine in the area. Those who frequented his pubs (many in the London end of Essex, but some scattered as far as Chelmsford and even Colchester) were treated to stay-backs whenever they wanted, safe in the knowledge that the local constabulary was unlikely to trouble them. Sometimes, for a treat, he would send a girl from one of his clubs down to entertain the locals by busting moves after hours. Just now and again, mind.

He also owned a titty-bar that was so sleazy and so scuzzy that you had to wipe your feet on the way out: this was where his staff had their Christmas social most years.

Whenever he was asked how he, the son of a Bermondsey car mechanic had achieved so much in just under sixty years, his answer was simple: teamwork.

Teamwork, and taking an interest. Keeping hands-on. It was a misconception that the rich simply hired other people to do things for them, preferring to spend their days sipping cocktails, playing tennis and spending their money (and cosily counting it of an evening).

It was a mistake for ambitious people to think like this, and while Layer rarely cashed up a till at the end of the night himself, he would know if any of his staff had had their fingers in it.

He also took great care in who he hired. Through his police contacts, he was able to run full background checks on all his 'dirty staff', thus ensuring that everyone he hired for muscle had at least had some dealings with the law. Anyone with a clean licence was either too slick (nobody wanted a clever thug) or they didn't have the right instincts.

Layer had also had the good sense to separate his 'dirty' staff, as he called them, from his regular (clean?) staff. Therefore he had a team of chefs, gardeners, mechanics and caddies and the like who wouldn't take a pen home if it didn't belong to them.

His roster housed several Technical and IT specialists who were prepared to break the law, just as long as it paid well and they didn't have to get their hands dirty.

He also had lawyers and accountants, and it was hard to tell which section they belonged to.

So he had a lot. And like anyone who had a lot, he had a lot to lose. But, as he told himself with a decent pull on his Havana Regal, it was fear of failure that made people think like this. And fear of failure was like any other fear –

it was a weakness that keeps you safe but ultimately holds you back, stops you taking risks; Norman Layer had decided long ago not to be held back by anyone or anything – especially not something as silly and as little as fear.

It had all started one Saturday morning more than forty years ago. A young Norman was helping out in his father's garage when two men came in with expensive suits and their chests puffed out, asking if they could 'speak to the old man'.

Norman took against these two *before* they started talking about protection money. So, he fetched a heavy-duty tyre iron and beat the two men half to death with it, working their shins, their knees and their ribcages until he needed to catch his breath and they could take no more.

His dad appeared halfway through the beating and looked on in astonishment, afraid to intervene in such a frenzied attack, but also afraid they would get another visit, and that this time it might from the boss himself. They would have done, too, had his boy not had the good sense to go and see the boss before the boss could come and see them.

Arthur Cramble had been a big player around London back in the days of the dancehalls – a real contender. He held on to his title, too – right up until the day when a local scamp burst into his office above the Bermondsey Palais with a tyre iron, only this time taking things a bit further and going for the head as well as the body. Cramble didn't feel too clever then, and neither did he a few days later when he got out of the hospital only to discover that his dancehalls had all burnt down, and so had his house. With his wife and his three children inside.

The only emperor this one-time Mr Big had anything in common with now was the late Roman emperor Nero; Cramble's empire had crumbled. He took his own life soon after, and Norman Layer's old man never paid for protection again.

He finished his cigar and took in his beautiful garden vista once more before walking back indoors, proud that someone from such humble beginnings had come so far and had achieved so much.

There was one person in the world Norman Layer was afraid of, but she spent most of her time with her personal trainer these days.

Chapter 8

Wednesday started better than Monday for Dave (Tuesday had started the same way, i.e. with a hangover, after Monday's impromptu jam session with Mick and Danny was followed by the traditional visit to the union bar), but only a little bit better. He hadn't woken up with a mouth like a birdcage and a head like John Bonham's kick drum, but he had been woken by a disturbing dream in which he'd been the victim of a gangland killing.

He'd been having this dream for about a year now, and it rattled him every time. On this occasion, he'd woken up as the final blow rained down (it was a deadly cosh of some kind, although he couldn't remember what it was exactly), but he wasn't always this lucky. Once, he'd experienced the whole thing, and lay dead yet somehow still conscious in total darkness for a period of time that was impossible to measure.

As Dave usually did when he was woken by this terrible dream, he'd sat up and smoked a couple of ciggies, resisting the temptation to wimp out and switch on his bedside light. He wished he could swap this dream permanently for the one involving Jennifer Aniston – or the other two, for that matter – and at least this thought brought out a half-smile, and he decided he was awake. Which was good, for he knew that if he went back to sleep with his head still in a dark place then he risked returning to the scene of the crime.

Then he got up and made some coffee, and for a time he sat in his kitchen, puffing away and wondering what he could do today.

He doubted that someone as delicate and as vulnerable as the Prof would have resolved his latest crisis yet, so there would be no lectures to attend. Thus Dave was left with what the middle-classes sometimes called an 'open window'.

Maybe he'd go and kick a ball around the park. Yes, he liked that idea a lot.

Dave was at university on an Arts Council scholarship, awarded to him in recognition of his 'musical excellence' (he was very good on harmonica, and no slouch as a singer, either) and his 'commitment to Afro-American and minority music forms' (he played a lot of blues and a tiny bit of jazz, which seemed to tick the right boxes).

And as he often reflected, he was helping the university send out the message that their doors were now open to the working classes (and they were just waiting for their tuition fees to come rolling in, too).

Certainly, Dave felt like this when, three days into the course, he was selected for a radio interview by the university's marketing department, and he was encouraged to drop his 'aitches' and throw away the letter 't' as often as he saw fit. All good for the new, inclusive era of higher education, he imagined it had been decided somewhere along the corridors of power.

He'd been sceptical about starting life as a mature student (and whether there was such a thing, after Freshers' Week), but as time went by, he found some of the people there were decent enough, and he'd started to feel at home. And, in the case of Daniel Blyth and Mick Davies, he'd also made a couple of good friends (something he didn't do easily).

There was no escaping, however, the vast cultural difference between Dave and most of the other students; he was cut from tougher cloth, basically, and it stood out, too, no matter how many times they'd all been told otherwise.

Seven years earlier, the incoming prime minister came up with a ruse to boost his popularity. Simply, he told the people of Britain their country no longer has a class system, or that at least it was on its way out – Britain was set to become a 'classless society', don't you know! Yes, the new boss was calling time on the upstairs/downstairs arrangement of old (something that in Dave's opinion was a) already on the wane anyway, and b) quite capable of doing away with itself had people actually wanted it to).

If Dave smelt a rat when he heard this, then he damn nearly choked when he saw a picture of the new premiere in one of the red-top newspapers (there was always one of those on the site) cosied up with a guitarist from a popular band of the time. This was a band who, along with a rival band from Dave's adopted hometown of Colchester, had made it 'cool' to be British – or more specifically, British working-class – again. The groovy PM had seen this, and he wanted some of it, badly.

Sadly, it was all a lie. Dave knew this because as well as laying bricks himself, he'd grown up seeing his father's hair turn grey right in front of his eyes, and had often wondered if his old man would live to be an old man.

Dad often told him that manual work was good for the soul. Which might be true, but Dave knew it wasn't always good for your back; Don Hunter's back was buckled by the time he was forty, and his poor knees were knocking as he hobbled back from the pub nearly every night. This wasn't how Dave wanted to go, and so he pursued a career as a musician, initially playing gigs at night and 'working construction', as the Americans called it, by day. He gained some recognition as well: he made a couple of CDs, supported a few named artists and he had had a residency at some London clubs.

Then came the offer to study at the prestigious Anglian University CMA: Dad would have been so proud if he wasn't dead.

Some of the folks back home labelled Dave as a traitor, of course, and accused him of 'jumping ship', or 'switching sides' etc., but Dave knew he would just have to accept this. Now, he was fourteen months away from having letters next to his name – which was better than the criminal record his old headmaster had predicted.

Just as he was thinking this, Dave's mind went back to the old 33⅓ rpm 12-inch wax cylinder that was still sitting on his turntable from Sunday, and the dusty, dog-eared sleeve he'd taken it out of. He thought about Bobby Fulton, the artist whose smoky rasp filled the disc's grooves so effortlessly. Why had he never heard of him? Why had Fulton vanished from the scene?

In Dave's mind, there was something odd about this. Once you cut a record, he thought, that was *it,* right? *You* were it. You didn't just disappear, that was for sure. If the album didn't sell many copies, you went back to having nothing to lose and got on with it. That's what Wilko said, the time Dave met him after a blistering set at the Kursaal a few years back.

Dave kind of knew this already, but it was nice to have it confirmed by a true master – i.e. the valuable lesson that a musician's life was never more than a work in progress. Scoring hit records was an enviable achievement, of course, and he'd call anyone who said otherwise a liar. Who wouldn't want to see their picture on the cover of the Rolling Stone?

But the real goal should be to better yourself artistically, professionally and musically. That was how you kept going when you played to one man and his dog and half a dozen ashtrays, and how you coped with drunks who requested bullshit songs by Robbie Williams, only to become aggressive when you politely declined, wasn't it?

Dave also knew that quality players didn't just disappear, they never quit. They took the highs with the lows, the good with the bad and the glitter with the gutter, but they didn't quit: they didn't have it in them to quit.

Maybe he would give the album another spin later. He noticed that while he'd been deep in thought, the sun had risen and morning had broken. Dave swapped his Homer Simpson slippers for a pair of Nikes and headed for the park.

Over in his Chigwell mini-mansion, Norman Layer put the phone down on his last consultation of the night that had now turned to day again and decided it was time to get some rest. He relieved his two aides, knowing he would meet them again in less than forty-eight hours.

There were two other agencies involved in what he was planning, and he had spies in both camps. Both of these men were risking theirs and their family's lives by talking to him like this and passing on the information they did, and they charged him a high price for doing so. They both suspected that they too were being watched, and they were right to think this; each of them was being carefully shadowed by members of Layer's gang who had gotten in with their respective firms several months earlier.

Not that Mr Layer suspected any treachery, of course; they knew what he was capable of, after all. Plus, he knew that he could trust them. These were the kind of men that would take their secrets to their graves – he would make sure of this once the job was done.

Norman Layer knew that planning was everything. Planning and being able to think on your feet when something went wrong.

Because something *always* went wrong.

Chapter 9

Dave had just got back from his early morning kickabout when the phone rang.

"'Allo mate!"

He recognised the voice instantly. It belonged to one Mick Warren, otherwise known as –

'Dirty' Mick, 51

Dirty Mick was the owner of a rather pokey little entertainment agency. On the surface, and indeed in Yellow Pages, it seemed fairly legit. They had a postcode and a landline number, but it didn't take Sherlock Holmes to work out that Star Quality Entertainment shared its address and its premises with a breaker's yard out near the old river town of Maldon. Near the entrance to the muddy yard was a little portacabin, where a short man with National Health specs and a raincoat was cooking bacon on a mini gas stove while talking on his mobile. This was the office.

"What ya' got?" said Dave.

If his response seemed blunt, then it was meant to: lower forms of life needed to know who's boss.

"I've got you a weddin' gig over in Furrock. It's in the backroom of a nice little pub just off the taahn centah."

Dirty Mick's voice was nasal, raspy and treacly, and you didn't have to see him to want him locked up.

"Okay," said Dave. "When?"

"I'm glad you asked," said Mick. "It's this Friday – farrve 'undred, cash in 'and. My cut'll be in the envelope. Bring it round 'Monday, and the rest is yours."

"I'll phone the others and let them know. I can't see it being a problem – they'll appreciate the work at this time of year."

So will I, come to think of it.

Dave thought this, but he didn't say it; he had vowed long ago never to show gratitude to a man of such poor taste and low standards as Dirty Mick.

78

"I'll get the details over in a flash. All they want is a nice little groop for some dancin' with a few arse-grabbers later in the evenin' – you'll be home before you know it."

Click.

Dave wasted little time on small talk, even with people he did like. Right now, he needed to shower – partly because he'd been running, but mostly because talking to Dirty Mick made you feel like that.

Nobody had ever been able to tell Dave how Mick had earned his 'dirty' moniker. Dave had mulled it over, and as he could see it, there were three possibilities:

First up, he certainly was unclean (fucking disgusting in fact, with his chip-pan hair and grimy, dirty jacket), but this was too obvious.

Brushing this all-too-easy theory aside, Dave had wondered if it had something to do with his sexual practices. There was no choice but to reject this idea since anyone who looked and sounded (and, dear God, smelled) like Dirty Mick did would not have got it within 100 yards of a female in a very, very long time. Even if he paid for it, she'd still have to find it underneath all that greasy flab of his.

So the only other possibility Dave could see was that it must be something to do with the fact that he wore his raincoat all year round.

And that was too upsetting to think about.

Dave was grateful for the gig, though. The thawing-out period of the year – i.e., roughly the first three months of it – could be a graveyard shift for musicians, and this one had been no exception. Plus, the good folks at the Inland Revenue would be busy now, what with all those late tax returns to sort through, so it wouldn't be right to add to their workload, would it?

No, it wouldn't, and Dave and his bandmates would hang on to the money like the decent souls they were.

It saddened Dave that so many people nowadays

didn't show the same consideration that he did, and had forgotten the simple truism that a little bit of kindness goes a long way.

He'd call the others later – there was no great hurry.

The shower and the preceding run left him feeling refreshed and renewed, with all thoughts of his agent having gone down the plughole and into the sewer where they belonged. Now casually dressed in blue jeans and an old T-shirt bearing an iconic 1957 Chuck Berry movie poster, he got a cold Bud from the fridge and perched himself on his kitchen stool. Dave had recently caved in to peer pressure and bought one of these mobile phones that so many people had these days. He hated them, but he also hated owning things and not using them.

"'Allo Mick, how ya' doin', mate?"

This was Mick Davies – not the dirty one Dave had spoken to a moment ago.

"'Allo Dave, you alright, mate?"

"Fancy earning a one-er?"

"Count me in. I'll call Danny."

"Nice one," said Dave. "It's Friday night. Briefing's at my place at twenty-one-hundred-hours tomorrow. Bring a bottle."

This time the 'click' was more of a 'bleep' – far from Dave's favourite sound.

Showing great restraint, Dave sipped his Bud as opposed to draining it in two quick chugs like he sometimes did after a gig or a band practice.

It was still early. Too early for beer, some would say. But then what was life if you couldn't live a little dangerously?

In fact, as Dave would soon find out, he was about to start living very dangerously.

He'd meant to give the mystery record another spin for some time now, or even flip it over and see what was on side two. He took a 'sup'(longer and more satisfying than a sip, but not as reckless and gratifying as a full-blown chug) of Budweiser and decided now was the time.

On the way to his record deck, he stopped to get his cigarettes. And, of course, another cold one.

Chapter 10

If Norman Layer was a moment late for his meeting, then it was unlikely he would face any questions as to why – it was simply one of the perks of being the boss.

All the men he'd sent for were present and correct, he was pleased to see, and they were all wearing the specified clothing: black T-shirts, running tops (handed over at the door, also black) and pocketless black running trousers.

They had been picked up by one of his mechanics, a trustworthy and reliable man named Ron Butler who was keen to earn some extra cash doing some small driving jobs on the side (and one rather big job, he would soon find out).

The men had been dropped at separate points along an invisible perimeter line each within a three-mile radius of the clubhouse. From there, they went the rest of the way on foot along a carefully charted course; each had their own route, a map of which had been sent with their invitations just days earlier, along with strict instructions for the recipients to memorise then destroy them.

Upon arrival they had given their running tops to an aide who, after a thorough pat-down had sent them through to the conference area, each of them making the correct assumption that their return journey would be carried out in a similarly covert fashion.

Handily, one of the aides was a bit of a technical wizard and had managed to cause a glitch in the club's CCTV system the previous night: the meeting had never happened.

Throughout his career, many people had told Norman Layer he was overly cautious, that he was obsessive, paranoid even. Most of them were now sewing mailbags or watching their backs every time they showered. Or they were dead.

With the curtains drawn and the conference area

dimly lit, Norman Layer stepped up to the ramp.

He was six feet two and slim, and he moved with slow, effortless grace. As gentlemen of a certain vintage were taught to, he looked upwards and wore a smile. It was a thin smile, however, and it suggested not warmth but cruelty. His stony face was a good deal longer than it was wide, and he had a tidy wedge of silvery hair up top and a granite jaw below. He also had dark, narrow eyes that could have belonged to a hawk or a raven.

He avoided the usual gangster attire – pork pie hats, gold medallions, leopard-skin coats, etc. – because he was a leader, an original, and therefore he saw no need to copy others. Norman Layer wore what wanted, and right now he was wearing a black polo neck tucked into cream slacks, and a pair of black leather shoes that didn't have much of a shine.

"Gentlemen," he said. "Thank you for being here at this ungodly hour, and I apologise for this and for any other inconvenience. But, as we all know, due diligence must be observed and all the rest."

There were five of them in total – five of the meanest, toughest and most sinister-looking hoodlums you'd ever see. In addition to Slouch and 'Left-Handed' Pete, there was:

'Shark', 56

As well as a short spell in the armed forces, Shark had served several much longer spells in prison. He was similar to Slouch in size and appearance (albeit with a bigger waistline), and the two of them had worked together before – on a couple of big jobs, actually. Slouch remembered that Shark was a horrible fucker who didn't care who got hurt, just as long as someone did. (Slouch hadn't exactly been champing at the bit to work with him again, either.)

The story behind Shark's name wasn't a nice one; he often showed his teeth, and he sometimes used them.

The story was that he was once sent to break a man's fingers in what should have been just a routine interrogation. But the man in question had had spirit, and he spat in Shark's face as the questioning started. His fingers didn't get broken that day, but only because Shark opened his jaws and bit several of them off.

The only good thing to come from this was that the subject gave a full confession there and then; he came clean, and he was unlikely to put his remaining digits in the till in the future.

Frankie Howse, 61

Stepney-born, gipsy-blooded Howse was an illegal boxer and one of Norman Layer's top debt collectors. He was six-foot-seven, and he had a frame like a gorilla, but he was much, much cleverer than one.

Having made his name in the murky world of prizefighting, where he was considered both royalty and legend, Howse joined the organisation somewhat late in life. He'd proved his worth on several occasions, but he was still regarded as a newbie by certain members of the group.

The line-up was completed by a retired Welsh Guard. His name:

Barry Wise, 54

Wise had a talent for making people empty tills and open safes very quickly indeed. The reason – his threats to kill were more than just threats, and most people could see this. Most, but not all, sadly.

Barry had spent the early part of his life in Liverpool, something his mixed accent – part lilting Valleys, part guttural Scouse – betrayed accurately. He wore a thick moustache, which gave off a military air as well as the slightest hint of homosexuality, although you'd be wise not to say so.

"All my life," Norman Layer said, "I have never been a man who enjoys a challenge. I have also never backed *down* from a challenge." He paced the room to dramatic effect. "And this is because, gentlemen, as I see it there *are* no challenges – just opportunities."

His goons wondered what he was building up to, except for Slouch and 'Left-Handed' Pete, who simply wondered *what* he was up to.

The boss often started out with a motivational speech like this; he had charisma, showmanship, even, as people who were born to lead often did. No one could take their eyes off him, and it would have been foolish to do so.

"And it is this positive mental attitude that has made me the man I am today." This was followed by a five-second pause in which he made eye contact with all of the men present or at least he seemed to. Usually, this meant the good bit was coming.

"We are men of means – *distinguished* gentlemen, no less – who have made our mark while others have just made their way: we chose to lead, not follow."

He broke off the stare, which was of some relief to Slouch and 'Left-Handed' Pete and most likely the other three. "Sadly, gentlemen, all good things must come to an end. None of us is getting any younger, even though some of our wives do seem to be." This was met with a very small burst of very nervous laughter from the audience. "That's why it is important for us to go out with a bang and that we end things in a befitting manner."

Though he was unlikely to give chapter and verse on the subject, Norman Layer had a firm grasp of the mechanics of propaganda.

He used the word 'we' several times in his address, but he used the word 'I' more frequently just in case anybody got the wrong idea.

People needed to feel they stood a chance of improving their lot in life or they would simply stand still and wait to die. That, or they'd fuck off and work for a rival outfit.

Layer had noticed on his first (and last) trip to America many years earlier that service staff there could not do enough for you. When he'd remarked on this back home, he'd been amazed to find that a great many Brits believed this was because the Americans were better natured than the British.

Rubbish, Norman had thought correctly. Either they wanted a tip, or they believed that if they sold more doughnuts than the person at the next counter they might become manager one day.

It was a lie, but it was an effective one.

By the same token, Norman Layer also knew that while it was important not to be seen to pull up the drawbridge altogether, it was just as important to keep the house in order and make sure no one had any illusions as to who was the boss. He had seen what *that* could lead to.

Having decided his troops were sufficiently impressed, Layer started unveiling his plan. It went like this: for the last year, with the help of some spies, Layer had been monitoring the activities of the renowned 'Cleaver Gang', a drug gang from Deptford, South London. Over the last ten years or so, this family-run unit had taken control of nearly all of London's drugs supply.

They had started out running a few London nightclubs, but this was simply for practical purposes; they had no real interest in the licensed trade, and they hadn't needed to have, either. Being the new kids on the block, brothers Alex and Samuel Cleaver always knew that the real profit, the real power, came from fine white powder. Or just the cheap shit that a 1970s guitar hero wouldn't have put within several feet of his nose yet did such brisk business in the region's nightclubs.

The Cleavers didn't like getting their hands dirty, a point Mr Layer was keen to impress on his audience. This was partly to air his disgust at these college boys trying to pick up his mantle, but more to make his men feel at ease about the people they would be double-crossing and bankrupting (and quite possibly condemning to death, once news of their supposed theft had travelled up the pipeline to their suppliers).

Like any drug gang, the Cleavers used heavies – often armed heavies – to prevent exactly the kind of thing Norman Layer had planned for them. Where Layer had the advantage, however, was that he knew every detail of the Cleavers' plan.

Through his sources, Layer knew that the gang collected a twice-a-year shipment of Bolivia's finest from a variety of spots along the South East coast. Wisely, they never used the same place twice.

Their next pick-up was arranged for in the small

hours of the May Day bank holiday (still some months away), from an unmanned jetty in a secluded stretch of Kent coastline. A luxury cruiser would be bringing in three tons of the stuff to be collected by employees of the Cleavers. If nobody saw, and if they got away with it, the two brothers would net themselves a cool 60 million and retire within a year while still the right side of forty. That was where this lot came in.

The Cleaver's men (there would be five in total) wouldn't make the collection – they wouldn't even make it to the location. Instead, they would be ambushed, beaten and terrorised before being locked in the boot of one of two falsely registered cut-and-shuts supplied by Norman's mate, Mick, from out in the sticks. They would see daylight again, but they wouldn't be feeling too chipper when they did, and they would have some serious explaining to do once they'd hitch-hiked their way back to HQ.

Layer's men would take the rival gang's vehicles

and go to the drop-off under the guise of the Cleaver's men, where they would relieve the skipper and his crew of their bounty in exchange for a message for their boss, should they be brave enough to report back to him. Their message was that he could, on behalf of the Cleaver brothers, go and fuck himself. And if they wanted to put up any kind of a fight, well then more fool them.

Slouch and co. would then load up the stolen cars (thankfully, the Cleavers were smart enough to realise that vans driving fast, in convoy at three in the morning could look suspicious) with the stolen shipment and head for the border. Back in the county, they would swing by the clubhouse to unload the gear and then tear across to Maldon where Dirty Mick would put the cars in the crusher, all before sunrise.

"And then," Layer continued after a pause, "we'll meet back here for a celebratory breakfast, courtesy of the house and prepared by my head chef."

To Slouch, this seemed like a strangely civilised and frankly crazy way to end a job. Had the boss forgotten how long it takes your nerves to settle after a stunt like this? Or how long it sometimes takes to get your pulse under control, or how it could sometimes be two or three days before the adrenalin stopped pumping and you could do normal things like eating, sleeping or maybe even go to the khazi again?

He's fucking lost it, Slouch thought.

He was right to think this, too. It was unlikely that anyone would be in the mood for a hearty breakfast after the kind of job Layer was talking about. Not after cheating death twice in one night (when guns are carried, they are always used). Not after doing over two lots of heavies, then driving at speed across two counties in a vehicle registered to known criminals, while carrying enough guns and cocaine to get you put away for life – no way.

As for 'Left-Handed' Pete, well, he found all of this

a bit strange, too. His main concern was that Mr Layer had used the word 'we' in the bit about meeting for a celebratory slap-up afterwards. Did this mean the boss was coming with them? It had certainly sounded like it, and he didn't like the idea of that at all.

It was a known fact that Norman Layer had not been on a job himself for many years (and with a team like this he hadn't needed to, either). It was a well-thought-out plan, but was this really for someone who plays golf four times a week?

This was the question in 'Left-handed' Pete's mind.

Both men knew it wasn't the done thing to share doubts, and especially not in such esteemed company. This didn't make them go away, though.

Frankie Howse also picked up on these points – not that his poker-faced expression would have shown it; to him, these were just minor niggles or small points. He was, as his boss had said earlier, a man of means, and a practical man. Practical men know that problems don't get solved by worrying, and just as the boss could see opportunity where other men saw a challenge, Frankie Howse only bothered with solutions when problems arose.

Barry Wise and Shark, on the other hand, were delighted at the prospect of banging a few heads together and maybe even pointing a gun at someone again. Then they found out they had to have their tattoos removed before the job.

Chapter 11

"He's started early," said Dave, when he saw Danny waving at them from across the street, wearing a Tommy Cooper hat and a silly grin, among other things.

Mick parked his Ford Transit close to the curb where Danny stood. Without any instruction, Danny slung his kit bag in the back of the van, then walked round to the front and got in next to Dave. A merry "What ho!" confirmed that he had indeed been on the syrup already.

Danny was one of those strange people who could play an instrument while blasted. If anything his playing got better with drink, whereas Dave preferred to remain sober as a judge. Well, he'd have a pint or two on account of where he came from (you can take a boy out of Essex…), but he knew when to stop.

Mick, poor bugger, usually had to drive. Danny lived in agreeable Lexden on the western outskirts of town, and it only took Mick three minutes to get on the London road from there.

They hit the A12 around five pm, just as the evening rush hour was gathering pace. The road was busy, but speed and progress were good in both directions.

To Dave, there was something energising, magical even, about a rush down a motorway in the late dusk. The roar of a hundred engines, the smell of tyres and exhaust fumes mixed with the excitement of the night just waking made him feel alive in a way that he would struggle to put words to.

As a kid, in his dad's works van, Dave had often been mesmerised by the river of traffic lights that bobbed and flowed in the other direction, and though he wouldn't admit it (not to this lot, anyway), he still felt it now, just a little bit. He looked up and saw the dim, distant flickering of a jet plane's tail-light, no doubt coming in to land at Stansted or maybe Heathrow, and in his mind he drew the faces of the people on board, waiting to land and get home to see some friendly faces. Soon be home and dry, he told them silently. For you never lost that sense of wonder. However hard you tried, and no matter how hard the modern 'grown-up' world tried to force you to give it up, you never could or would.

He was startled back to earth as Mick tried to change lanes near Hatfield Peverel. A man going too fast in a BMW and already in the outside lane didn't like this and hit his horn. Then Mick fought fire with fire and hit the horn himself before winding his window down and doing what only seemed right. Danny leaned across and patted Mick's shoulder to show his support.

"Good on ya, son. You tell 'im!" said Dave, also wanting to support his friend.

The incident came as a great relief to Danny, for whom the hushed silence had been almost deafening. There was no way he was going to let it creep back, either.

"Did you know your favourite person was kicking up a stink about old Rolphy missing classes the other day?" he said to Dave, letting Mick concentrate on driving for the moment.

"Who's that?" asked Dave.

"Oh, come on, you know who: a certain *Miss Adcock.*"

"Let me guess," said Dave. "She stormed up to the Students' Union and started raising her voice and waving her arms around? Made it sound like some kind of human rights violation, did she?"

"They say she was there nearly four hours," said Mick, deadly serious.

"At one point they had to threaten to call security," said Danny.

Dave shook his head. Guess she's still mad at them for 'rigging the vote' at the last election, he thought but for some reason didn't say.

"So then, Dave," said Mick. "What happened with you and her?"

Dave had been asked this many times, and he was starting to tire of it. His account had been truthful but in no way fruity or controversial. And therefore not good enough.

It was rumoured he'd been overheard in the SU bar one night, well-oiled and engaged in some rather juvenile wordplay involving her name. Or more specifically, her second name. Which has the word 'cock' in it. This wasn't true, and Dave would never have stooped this low even though he could see that the possibilities were endless. Other people on campus said that she and Dave got it on once but fell out afterwards, and if Dave ever found out who had started that one he would take their tongue out with pliers.

Sadly, these rumours were neither true or the cause of hers and Dave's bitter feud. The cause of this went deeper than something Dave may or may not have said or something he definitely didn't do.

Dave, you see, didn't like this Adcock lady very much. He didn't like the way she interpreted everything as a grave and serious affront to something or other. She seemed to want to fight 'oppression' even when there was none (and there usually wasn't any, either).

He also disliked and criticised people who claimed to hold 'anti-establishment' values while attending a higher education facility owned by the establishment that he or she purports to oppose. Dave had tried to make his peace with her, 'cos he was that kind of guy, but sadly it was to no avail. She was hard to pacify, this Adcock lady, always up for an argument. Dave thought this was strange for someone who couldn't go more than three minutes without talking about the Iraq war and the need for peace in our time, but mostly he let it slide – mostly.

"I suppose you clocked the American playing the perfect gent with your bird the other night?" Mick asked

105

him.

Dave sighed. "I wondered when this would come up," he said.

"Mate, it's fine if you don't wanna talk about it."

The usual pre-gig high spirits seemed to drift out of the window that was still open from Mick's road-rage incident a moment ago.

"Fuck it," said Dave. "It'll be whatever it'll be. Que se-fucking-ra."

Dave had chosen not to confide in his college friends about his unrequited romantic interest, the certain girl he'd been in love with a long, long time, and he felt he had a good reason for keeping quiet about this.

Dave was older and wiser and therefore more worldly than these two. In the sixteen months or so that he'd known Danny and Mick, he had become something of a father figure to them. He was a kindly alpha male who wasn't afraid to tell Danny to shut the fuck up and slap him across the face if he got out of hand.

He took his role seriously, so he was reluctant to let them see the slightest chink in his armour even though they could see it anyway. Dave Hunter hated losing, but he especially hated people seeing him lose. And with the way things were going …

He could lose any day now.

"Still," said Danny, as he unscrewed the top on his hip-flask and took a hearty gulp, "there might be some bridesmaids there tonight looking to shame the family."

Good old Danny – you needed him sometimes.

"And God knows my family needs shaming."

Chapter 12

The lads' banter continued for fifteen minutes or so before the noisy backdrop of rain pounding the hood of the vehicle got the better of them, and they gave up. The light drizzle that had accompanied the first part of their journey became torrential, so conversation became impossible, and now the three amigos sat in the van saying nothing at all. In fact, Danny was having a little snooze, perhaps because he was bored but more likely because he'd been drinking all afternoon.

He wouldn't be dozing for long. Exactly one hour after they left Colchester, Mick and Dave saw the sign for Thurrock and Grays through Mick's misted-up windscreen: they were nearly there.

Thurrock was a mini-county within the county of Essex, and Grays was a town at the coastal end of it. The local tourist board didn't do much to promote it as a seaside town because Thurrock and Grays didn't have a tourist board.

Dave gave Danny a nudge that was more like a thump. "Look alive, Danny boy – we're 'ere!" he said.

Dave insisted they always travelled light. He couldn't afford roadies at this stage, but he didn't want musicians doubling for them either. Therefore Mick's amplifier of choice was a 60-watt Fender valve combo that he could lift with one hand. Dave had a battered brown leather briefcase for his 'gob-irons' – that's his harmonicas – and a Revox tape machine to help him capture the sound of the first British blues movement, Stones, Pretty Things, Yardbirds, etc.

Danny took an electric organ along to gigs, but only in case the pub didn't have a piano, or in case the pub had a piano that was in such poor condition he would consider it beneath him to play it. Luckily, neither was often the case.

The PA system and the microphones usually arrived

with the 'first cavalry', two old mates of Dave's from Southend who usually arrived an hour before the others (Dave was a stickler for detail). Their names were Nicky and Ricky, and they travelled to gigs in a white van similar to the one Mick used to bring in the auxiliaries.

Nicky and Ricky were two old warhorses who seemed to have been around forever. Certainly, they had backed visiting American blues artists back in the 60s, when guys like John Lee Hooker and Sonny Boy Williams got news of their British blues impersonators – Clapton, Page, Beck etc. – and came over here to show them how it was done.

Nicky and Ricky had kept photographic reminders of their swinging sixties heyday, and a young Dave had been blown away by their scrapbooks. The Crawdaddy, Eel Pie Island, Klooks Kleek … These guys had played them all.

Now, as then, they were a rhythm section for hire –

they were a good one, too. With Nicky behind a five-piece Ludwig jazz kit and Ricky's low-slung bass grooves, you could think you were hearing Booker T and the MG's if it wasn't for Danny's 'pub Joanna' taking the place of a cool Hammond organ.

As ever, Ricky would be paid an extra hundred quid for supplying and operating the PA system tonight.

Danny and Mick used to think Dave was crazy for sharing out the profits like this, but they soon saw the advantages of being freed up to focus on the playing and of staying rested until it was time to hit.

Indeed, Mick and Danny had learned a lot from Dave, their 'elder', as it were. Initially, they were puzzled by his minimalist approach in an era when drummers constructed kits the size of Range Rovers and squashed them up against guitar amps of equally excessive size and volume. This kind of thing had become all the rage in recent years, and Dave hated it, wanted it stopped immediately. He explained to Mick and Danny that amplifiers were invented so that musicians could be heard in places like The Royal Albert Hall (two if you include trying to be heard above the dreadful din produced by the likes of Ginger Baker or John Bonham or the countless idiots they inspired). In a pub or small theatre, Dave told them, this was not only unnecessary but also counterproductive since anything louder than 90 decibels can damage people's hearing. And when a band plays loudly enough to damage people's hearing, it's unlikely that the skill and nuance of the players would shine through.

Danny and Mick had listened to Dave and given his methods a try. Now he had one of the best working bands in the country because two people had listened to a few words from the wise.

It was colder than the North Pole outside Leggero's, a

popular Grays nightspot doing a slow trade tonight on account of the biblical downpour and the biting gales that ripped along the Thames Estuary at this time of the year. Yet the wind and the rain went almost unnoticed by the two old bruisers on the door – almost. Hard men like these didn't whine that they were freezing their bollocks off – it just wasn't done. But there wasn't a man alive who wouldn't have preferred to have been indoors on a night like this, sipping a malt near a roaring fire or maybe even sharing a moment of cosy intimacy with his good lady wife.

Or in Slouch's case, paying £25 for an hour with a cheap, slutty hooker.

The pavement across the street was sprayed as a wave broke against the seawall next to it.

"Just look at it out there," said 'Left-Handed' Pete, in awe of Mother Nature at the height of her powers. Another wave crashed.

"I'm 'alf expectin' Noah's Ark to come up the estuary," he said.

Slouch thought about this for a moment. "Probably be full o' cocaine," he said, and both of them laughed.

"That or a load of East Europeans," said 'Left-Handed' Pete.

They laughed again, but not for very long. A brief silence fell and then it was business as usual.

"I 'fink itz a bleedin' liberty," said Slouch.

"Wot iz?" asked 'Left-Handed' Pete even though he knew the answer.

" 'Boss man making me get rid o' my tattoos like that."

"Well I hate to say it, but I think it's a good idea – I'm just surprised he didn't do it soonah," said Pete, not facing his friend as he didn't want to take his eyes off the street.

"Mighta' known I could count on you for support,"

said Slouch.

"Listen," said Pete, "I am not gonna live aaht my days in Dartmoor just because you wanted to keep the name of some dead mutt next t' yer elbah!"

This hurt Slouch about as much as a man like him could be hurt. It wasn't just his dog, either. There was Mum, Dad, two sets of grandparents, several uncles, his ex-wife (she could go, come to think of it), his estranged son, his blood group and his special forces logo ... Most of his upper body was decorated with ink tributes to his life and times. It had been quite a life too, one of peaks and troughs, highs and lows, and adventure. Now he would have to sit back while someone took a scalpel to all of his memories just because Norman Layer said so.

Neither Slouch or 'Left-Handed' Pete liked what they had heard this morning. Norman Layer could have retired years ago – his sons could have taken over the business while he sailed away to a life of luxury. He had his house, his holiday homes abroad, his golfing lodge and his glamorous wife to make up for the trophies that his golfing hadn't brought him. He had cars, money, power, guts and glory ... He had it all. What more could he want?

The answer was simple: he wanted more. Norman Layer wanted more power and more money, and he'd worked out that the way to get it was to run a bunch of low-lives out of town and become the biggest cocaine dealer in the country. To a man like him, it was worth risking the consequences of a bungled mission – in this case, death or a long spell in prison.

'Left-Handed' Pete would have preferred it if the boss had stuck to his golf and his Bentleys and taken the easy life. Slouch, on the other hand, had a different set of concerns entirely.

Slouch had hurt people all his life. Not with the same sickly relish as men like Shark or Frank Howse, but Slouch had been able to get the job done when it was necessary. He preferred it when it hadn't been necessary though, and people handed the drugs/keys/money over like he asked. This was the professional way of course, and jobs did go more smoothly if nobody tried anything. But lately, professionalism alone wasn't making Slouch hope and pray that more jobs would go like this.

He didn't regret forcefully removing junkies and sex pests from *Leggero's* and other premises over the years, sometimes taking them down to the seafront or an alleyway if an extra lesson needed teaching, but he had gone off roughing people up of late. His heart wasn't in it anymore, and this was only half the problem.

Recently, Slouch had experienced feelings of guilt about some of the things he'd done in the past. He knew he could never speak of this, and he could usually block it out – but not always.

Another wave exploded against the seawall and drenched a passing van.

Chapter 13

Dave liked a nice, clean venue. He liked a spacious set-up

area for the band with parking nearby and porter staff to

help. He especially liked having his own dressing room

with some lovely food and drink (courtesy of the host,

natch) and a pretty girl to show him to it.

Not that Dave didn't like to mingle – far from it, in

fact. Especially when the guests were charming, polite and

respectful (for he was quite a charmer himself, don't y'

know).

Oh, what pleasant company he'd thought on the rare

occasions when these reasonable wishes were met. Sadly,

tonight wasn't quite like this.

When Dave got out of the van, he noticed that

Nicky's van was parked away from the entrance to the

venue, and was presumably unloaded and locked up. This

meant the two brothers had arrived and were running to

schedule.

As Dave, Danny and Mick made their way to The Sea Wall Inn's front entrance, they came upon two unkempt, burly-looking chaps in dirty boots and navvies jackets, each with scraggly (but not long) hair. They were sitting on a bench next to the door as though they were performing sit-down sentry duty.

A gentleman by nature, Dave tipped an invisible cap to them with an amenable "evening chaps," but was met with silence, which he found rather strange and a bit fucking rude, actually. Somehow Dave caught the gaze of the biggest of the two chaps, and it was a blue-eyed, wolfish gaze that was rather less than welcoming. As Dave and his bandmates passed them the man muttered a sarcastic-sounding "Top o' the mahrnin' to ye."

Once they were inside the building, the scale of the trouble they were in became apparent, and Dave decided that if he lived to tell the tale, then Dirty Mick wouldn't.

For one thing, there was broken glass all over the wood planked dance floor. This did nothing to deter several of the women from kicking off their boots and dancing a crazed Celtic jig, and one lady was showing off her talent for standing on her big toe, to much applause.

The dancing was accompanied by an elderly man playing a lilting, triple-quaver melody on a penny whistle, with a lonesome Bohren drum for a rhythm section. The drum was beaten by a rough-hewn chap who looked to Dave like he'd be just as happy doing this with someone's head.

Dave's vision of violence was compounded by the sight of several of the pub's tables being used for impromptu arm-wrestling matches, and in one corner of the building two men were punching each other for fun.

The bride and groom were nowhere to be seen, but they didn't matter now, as it quickly dawned on Dave that their agent hadn't told them this was an Irish wedding.

The drink will flow, and blood will spill ...

Danny was first to speak: "I now pronounce you brother and sis –"

Dave slapped him so hard his cheek reddened (yet with such discretion that none of the revellers saw him do it, thankfully).

"Shut the fuck up," he told the whites of Danny's eyes.

"Shall we just get out now and sod the money?" asked Mick.

"Too late," said Dave. "Nicky and Ricky are here – we can't just leave them."

Nicky and Ricky were indeed already in the venue. They were set up and ready to play on the small stage at the back of the room (and thankfully near the fire exit), even though they knew the drill: get out at the first sign of trouble.

Silly fuckers.

There was nothing else for it, Dave thought. They would just have to grit their teeth and 'gut it out', as the Americans said. He told his friends this, and they began to wade through the mayhem and towards the stage, where they would be out of the way for a while but by no means in a place of safety.

Dave greeted Nicky and Ricky with a handshake each and put his battered, beloved briefcase down next to the middle mike stand, then gestured for Danny and Mick, standing either side of him to the left and right respectively, to get to work. Dave took the middle microphone partly because he was the most genial host of them all (but not a 'frontman' – Dave didn't like that term or the concept), but also because he knew from experience that if anyone wanted trouble, they would go to the man in charge. This way the others would have a chance to leg it and start the van.

In the same way that a captain at sea would go

down with his ship, Dave always put his bandmates before himself. Women and children were saved first aboard a doomed vessel, and because women and children were what musicians acted like most of the time, Dave Hunter tried to preserve this ancient, noble tradition.

Dave set out his harmonicas in order of their keys at the same time that Mick's guitar came out of its case. It was a shiny hollow-body Epiphone semi, the kind of guitar T-Bone Walker played on all those classic 50s cuts. As if this wasn't enough, Mick also had a Fender Telecaster that he kept open-tuned as did his beloved Keith Richards.

Dave never knew how 'Keef' got that *Honky Tonk Woman* sound, and he'd been impressed when Mick had shown him that by tuning two strings down by a tone and throwing one string away you could turn a guitar into a thing of savage beauty.

Thoughts of doing the thing Dave and co. came here to do, i.e. play some music seemed to take their minds off the dreadful situation they were in. Having set up quickly like the professionals they were, they retired to the bar.

They all bought a pint except for the drivers, and bar one incident where Dave had to stop Danny from telling another joke that could have got them killed, for a moment all seemed to be … Okay. Time passed as it did when gentlemen engage in banter, and at 9:00 pm they went to walk the boards, though really they were walking the plank.

This was where it all went horribly wrong.

With each band member in place, Dave opted to forego an introduction and counted the band straight in, using a two bar count-in as professionals do.

They started with a fast, swinging version of *Rock Around the Clock* – still a great song after fifty years. Dave sang a few verses before Mick perfectly replicated the fast solo performed on Bill Haley's original. Then Dave sang another verse before signalling for Danny to take a solo, knowing that with Danny's loose-fingered boogie their version could outstrip the original.

Deciding not to add some harmonica, Dave signalled for the end of the song. He didn't expect a standing ovation, but he wasn't expecting the eerie silence that greeted them either. He waited a second before counting in the next number: *Summertime Blues* by the late, great Eddie Cochran.

Dave couldn't help noticing that his band sounded good tonight, and was giving an above-average performance despite the unwelcoming atmosphere. This was how Dave knew – not believed, *knew* – live music should be, with the drummer and bass guitarist locked in and listening to one another (a rare skill these days), and the guitar and keys leaving space for each other and, again, *listening*.

Dave was almost enjoying it now, as he rolled out the words and the melody ever-so-slightly behind the beat in a way that was agony and ecstasy at the same time (a forgotten art in an era where producers foolishly used a 'click', believing every note had to be right on count). This could be happening after all.

Dave had learnt through guys like Nicky and Ricky that musicians should aim for consistency, the ability to shoot and score most times if not every time. That way you got hired, and if you had regular work, you could improve your chops while the rapport within the band grew. Then – and only then – one could reach the stage where a song with only three chords and a simple beat could become something magnificent right before your eyes. It was a thing to behold, and it was well worth the time and effort it took to achieve this.

And when the magic didn't quite happen? Well, because of that consistency that you'd worked for, you came away with your head held high and your reputation intact, knowing that you would get another chance.

But when it did happen, you felt your feet lift off the ground and an hour could feel like five minutes.

"I see Jamaica, the moon above," Dave drawled about half an hour in. *"I see the girl that I'm dreaming of!"*

He looked up to see that some people in the crowd were loosening up a little. The impromptu arm-wrestling continued as did the broken-glass jigs, but some feet were tapping, and a few glasses were raised.

"I take her in my arms and then, tell I her I love her near the end, with my Louie Louie!"

He was up and almost into it now, confident that as the evening progressed he could win them over and take them home. Then, something strange happened.

The sentry Dave had passed on his way in (he of the rugged apparel and lupine stare) came in through the door he'd been guarding a short time ago, followed closely by his friend. They stood motionless either side of the doorway, and even from the back of the room, the big fella

127

caught Dave's eye.

It was a cold stare that was as menacing as it was emotionless. Dave didn't scare easily, but for a second it was as though he was unaware of his surroundings, blind to the revellers in front of him and deaf to his bandmates behind him. He remembered the rule that the show must go on, even though tonight's gig put him in mind of The Rolling Stones at the infamous Altamont Festival, when Mick 'n' the boys had tried to play on as bloody scenes played out right before their eyes.

With The Rolling Stones in mind, Dave turned to his bandmates and called out for *Walking The Dog*, a floor-filler on countless nights before.

It didn't do badly tonight, either. Daring to look up again, Dave noticed people were up and into it. This was where he hit his stride, sometimes doubling Mick's guitar part on his Hohner blues harp. And play that riff Mick did, with Danny singing the chorus harmony part just like Brian

Jones did on this standout track from The Stones' first LP. All thoughts of the iceman disappeared as the song hit its high, and the final crescendo brought the curtain down on the evening's first performance or would have done if there was a stage curtain. There wasn't, but at times like this it didn't matter; the boys had done themselves proud.

Mick noticed the scary Irishman who was engaged in a staredown with his bandleader. He also saw something that Dave and the rest of the band hadn't.

Mick could see that for all the revelry, only half the people in the building seemed involved and willing to play. For every person high on the hog and wearing their best, there was someone with similar features to Dave's friend over by the door, and Mick quickly worked out that the split was a family one. He'd heard about this sort of thing before; now he was about to see it.

Dave, on the other hand, was still coming down from his rousing rendition and hadn't figured this out yet.

He wiped the sweat from his brow with an old beer towel and put his harmonica in its case, realising he'd forgotten the obligatory 'we'll be back soon so don't go no place' spiel. He turned to face the crowd and saw that the iceman had cometh again, and this time he was standing an inch from the stage and very much in Dave's face.

Chapter 14

At first, the Irishman stood there and said nothing at all. Dave, getting impatient now, decided he might as well see what he wanted and get it over with it. He'd resigned himself to the fact that things were going to get ugly so he saw no point in trying to put it off (he didn't know how ugly this was going to get, though).

Mick, on the other hand, knew exactly what was coming. He'd read the situation better than Dave and worked out that there was a historical grudge between the two families who were here tonight. All they needed was an excuse to try and settle it once and for all, and a barney involving a member of the band could be just the thing. Someone from the rival clan would intervene, which would reignite the feud and start a bloody, tribal battle. Which was what they were here for.

"Can I do something for you?" said Dave.

"I want you to sing Danny Boy," said the iceman, in a brogue so thick he could have been gargling porridge.

"Sorry – don't do requests," said Dave, unapologetically. He was careful to make eye contact with him for he knew you had to be firm with people like this, who could smell fear from a hundred yards, who knew one way to settle a problem and were still getting to grips with this whole standing upright business.

While this exchange went on, the pub's owner, a gentleman named Stanley Barrack, who wore a green tie on a green shirt and looked about forty, was out the back dialling 999. The operator asked if he wanted police, ambulance or fire brigade, and Mr Barrack told her she might want to send all three before slamming his phone down and getting his baseball bat out from under the stairs. "Not in my pub," he said as he jumped across the bar and made his way through the crowd.

"Oi don't tink yer listening to me," said Dave's

nemesis, still fixing him with a stare. "This is moy sister's wedding. Dad, God rest his soul is no longer with us, which means oi'm payin' for all dis," he said gesturing to the room.

"So y' see," he said as he ambled up onto the stage, crossing the line literally as well as metaphorically, "this means oi'm in charge. When oi say jump, you jump. D'ya hear me?"

As Dave listened to this, he noticed the big man's sidekick moving towards the fire escape, blocking the exit. Now there was nothing else for it.

His father taught him many years ago that attack was the best form of defence. If someone's acting like a c**t then treat them like one, Don Hunter used to say.

"You can fuck off an' all," Dave said to the empty space behind this c**t who thankfully was as stupid as he looked. He turned to see who Dave was talking to before he realised he'd been pranked. Dave slugged him hard with his right, certain the brute would go down.

But he didn't. He just spat out a mouthful of blood and went back to glowering at Dave, who noticed that the big man's slack-jawed grin revealed a row of blood soaked teeth.

"Oh, fuck off," was all Dave had to say to that before he swung at him again, and he heard a satisfying crunch as his fist connected with the big man's chin. If I could just get him off the stage, Dave thought.

Most of the guests were moving towards the stage now. There must have been sixty of them, all champing at the bit to see what would happen next.

From the corner of his eye, Mick saw the iceman's friend running towards him. Mick pretended not to see him until he jumped up on to the stage, then Mick picked his Telecaster up like a baseball bat and took his would-be attacker out at the knees.

Dave let out a full-blooded roar as he launched into

his enemy's waist in a rugby tackle. They crash-landed on the dance floor, and Dave heard something snap. Luckily, it was nothing of his.

Because Dave landed on top, he had an advantage over his adversary. He went to work, pounding him with both fists until he lost count of the punches he'd rained down on the ugly bastard's face. Then he stopped to catch his breath.

Big mistake. The big man's right hand sprang up and grabbed Dave's throat. This wasn't a hand that typed emails or wrote lecture notes. It was a callused, barnacled hand that swung hammers and dug ditches in winter, and it soon drained Dave of most of his strength and resolve.

The hand dragged Dave to his feet and continued the strangulation process with both men now standing. Dave tried to kick him in the bollocks but didn't have the strength for it. He clawed at the gorilla hand around his neck but gave up the ghost as he drifted towards unconsciousness.

Mick looked over to Danny, who nodded to confirm that it was time to go in and save their friend, and they both knew that this would be like kicking a wasp nest.

Danny got him first. He opened the big bastard's eyebrow with a left hook that would have floored and concussed a normal man. Sadly, this wasn't a normal man, and he didn't seem to feel a thing.

Mick knew they needed a plan. He looked over and saw that the fire exit to the right of the stage was clear (the man who had guarded it was off his feet and would be for some time, thanks to Mick's Telecaster). If he could free Dave from his mouth-breather opponent, he and Danny could march their wounded buddy to the nearest exit and perhaps get to the van. The ensuing melee could be just the distraction they needed.

So Mick set about freeing his friend who was showing vital signs for now at least. Deciding that blows to the head and body were a waste of time, Mick crept up behind their enemy and did something he didn't like and wasn't proud of: he crouched down, opened his right hand and clamped it shut on the big Irishman's testicles. Mick gritted his teeth and crushed as long and hard as he could, imagining his hand was a workshop vice.

A crowd gathered round to see this spectacle, and Mick thought this might bugger up his plan to escape amidst the chaos. His plan to set Dave free, however, was working, and the Essex strangler seemed to be loosening his grip.

Danny, ever the schoolboy, found the sight of Mick Davies with his hand round another man's genitals amusing and started to snigger, but he wouldn't be laughing for long. He saw four men with similar features and build to the one Mick was manhandling pushing through the crowd with serious looks on their faces. Correctly, Danny guessed they were the Irishman's brothers.

The crowd that had gathered nearby were also amused by what they saw. They whooped and hollered, and Mick hoped to goodness they were cheering for him.

The Irishman released his grip, and Dave hit the floor, seemingly out for the count. Mick took a chance and let go of the big man's squashed conkers, but it wasn't over yet.

"Trouble at high noon, Mick!" shouted Danny who was now preparing himself for grim battle. Impressed by Mick's resourcefulness earlier, he picked up the other guitar, the Epiphone semi-acoustic, and broke it over the head of the person nearest to him. One down and about fifty-seven to go, he thought.

This was when it hit the fan. Chairs flew, and glasses smashed. Women screamed, and men screamed. People with arms that could tear doors from their hinges took great chunks out of each other.

Dave came to and struggled to his feet. He couldn't

see his friends, couldn't make out much, in fact, but he could hear sirens outside, which was nice. Soon this will all be over, and I can have a nice cuppa, or maybe even a pint, he thought in the warmth of his delirium.

Then he said "Oh fuck," because saw that he was face to face with the man who had three-quarters throttled him a moment ago and who seemed oblivious to the battle royale that now raged around him.

"Call it a draw?"

He got no answer, just a big forehead crunching down on his nose. Now he was out for the count.

Chapter 15

"You should always eat a proper lunch. Otherwise, your tummy will shrink, and you won't eat your tea," so Dave's Aunt Reenie used to say.

Her husband Bert, Dave's late uncle, did just this. He ate three large meals a day throughout twenty-seven years of marriage, right up to his death from a massive heart attack three days before his forty-ninth birthday.

His auntie's words rang in Dave's ears now, as he looked suspiciously at his third luncheon at The Basildon and Thurrock Hospital. It was a bowl of ham and pea soup that made him wonder if he was quite as lucky to be alive as the doctor said he was.

Mick's was the first voice Dave heard upon coming to three days earlier. Mick didn't have much to say then, but he'd managed a few words to assure his friend that he was in good company.

As well as hoping for a sexy nurse to come and take his temperature, Dave hoped and prayed he'd see Mick in a 1950s American slapstick movie head bandage, with his leg in a cast suspended above his bed and an arm in plaster poking out to his side. And when Dave found the strength raise his head enough to look over at him (he'd given up trying to sit upright by then), he saw that Mick did have a leg in a cast – and he did too.

As for the sexy nurse, well that was a non-starter, but Dave decided this was probably for the best. He'd broken several bones, and he didn't want his heart going the same way.

He'd been unconscious for quite some time (two days, he found out later), and he needed to pass water in the same way that a blind man wants to see and he had a mouth like a camel market. Later that day, his doctor filled him in as to what had happened. The doc read out the notes the police had given him, and it seemed that the beating had carried on after Dave was knocked unconscious. Hence the broken leg, four cracked ribs and massive bruising to his head and upper torso, as well as the crunched, crooked septum and the messy bruise on his neck. And the two broken fingers on his right hand.

This was all news to Dave, who just remembered a big Irishman giving him a funny look, but his two broken fingers comforted him with the fact that he must have given as good as he got.

Oh well, worse things happen at sea he thought.

Then it hit him. Mick was in the bed next to his, accounted for and out of harm's way, but where was Danny? Dave assumed that Nicky and Ricky, being brothers, would have made their escape, but Danny? No, he was a musketeer, and he would have seen it through.

Dave called the doctor back and demanded to know where his friend was. The doctor told him Danny was fine and that they would see him soon. Dave believed him – he could always tell if someone was lying – but he was puzzled by Danny's absence.

Dave decided to not to take Aunt Reenie's advice. He was a long way from making a full recovery, so he was unable to summon the courage required to eat hospital food.

"Sorry, Aunt", he said as he put his spoon down.

By now Dave could tell which member of staff was approaching by the sound of their footsteps. The steps he heard now were firm and purposeful, and they clearly belonged to a man who knew what he was doing and where he was going: it was the doctor again.

As the doctor approached him, Dave noticed he had a certain spring in his step. Did he have good news? Was one of the nurses planning to swing by the off-licence after work?

The doctor stopped at the foot of his bed.

"I tried," said Dave, tilting his head to point his chin

at the soup.

"Sod that," said Doctor Chamberlain. "Get this down you, or you'll never get out of here." He took a Ginsters sausage roll from one of his jacket pockets and threw it to Dave.

Dave clapped his hands together and caught the snack. He did this instinctively but foolishly, and the pain that seared through his body a second later made his eyes water and took every ounce of breath from him.

"It's good news," said the Doc with a smile, about the only person around here who did, by the look of it. "By this evening you'll be ready for visitors."

This may have sounded nice, but Dave was less than elated. He was sure that at least one of these visitors would be from the local constabulary, wanting to know who, what, where, when and how and almost certainly not bringing grapes.

"I guess that's good news," said Dave, taking a

crafty bite from his Ginsters. "Cheers, by the way," he said.

"Don't mention it – or my name if Sister Pierce catches you with it. You should see her coming, mind. She's a big old girl, tough as old boots and about as glamorous."

Dave liked this cat. He was cool.

"Visiting time's at six," said the Doc. "Get some rest in the meantime. You want to look your best, don't you?"

Dave woke at around 5:45 pm and saw Danny walking down the middle of the ward, heading towards him. In his groggy state, nothing struck Dave as being odd about this. It was just Danny being his usual self, easy come, easy go. Dave just shut his eyes and tried to rest a little while longer. A second later he opened them and did a double-take.

"What the fuck?" he said.

Danny came to the foot of his bed, and Dave saw

145

that as well as being up and about there wasn't a mark on him.

"Hey, how come …?" was about as much as Dave could manage, and even that was more than Mick could. "You … You're … OK? Dave said.

"I'm fine thanks," said Danny. "Which is more than can be said for you. Ouch – that looks frightful."

"How come …?"

"Oh, I got out with Nicky and Ricky," said Danny. "Yeah, we got in the van. They dropped me off at the nearest train station, and I went straight home. No sense sticking around, bloody mess."

An awkward silence followed, and as ever Danny broke it albeit not in his usual fashion.

"I know I should have come sooner, but I felt so ashamed," he said with his head hung low. "Truth be told I could barely face seeing you both. And I didn't think you'd want to see me much either."

He kept his head down and spoke again after a lengthy pause.

"I think you should get someone else to play keyboards for you. Someone a bit more … Honourable, perhaps? Someone with a bit more backbone."

He still faced the ground, and Dave was first to try and talk him around. "Look, Danny, it's no –"

"No big deal? Well, it's a big deal for me – it's a bloody big deal, actually."

Danny was making eye contact now, and Dave thought this was a start since making eye contact meant pulling your head up; Dave knew he had to get Danny out of his rut and fast.

Danny continued. "Look, you're my best friends, and I left you for dead. What does that make me, eh?" It was a sincere moment, which was a rare thing with Danny. And he just had to over-egg it, didn't he.

"I've done enough," he said. "I should probably be

on my way." Danny made his bottom lip wobble as he said this, and spoke with an affected nasal tone for greater emotional resonance. This was when they sussed him out.

There was a brief silence, followed by a splutter from Mick, which Dave heard then had a little snigger himself. Then Dave's sniggering gave way to hearty laughter from all three of them, and the man in the bed opposite Dave's started laughing too.

The three amigos were back in business, and all was right with the world.

Danny had brought them presents: hip flasks topped up with expensive brandy that Dave and Mick accepted then hid when they heard a door open at the end of the ward. But it wasn't members of the hospital's staff that were coming to see them.

Several of Mick's relatives were there: his oldest brother Cliff and his wife, Sheila; his mum and dad, Clive and Rose; several uncles and aunts … It seemed as though the whole Davies family was there. A policeman followed them in, however, and he wasn't related to Mick – or Dave or Danny.

The rozzer was a serious-looking chap of about thirty, who stood at around six feet two. He walked up to Dave's bed then stopped and faced him intently.

"Don't get up," said the copper, which was the kind of humour Dave liked except for when he was the victim of it.

The young constable told Dave that this was just a routine visit. He told him he was there to see if he was alright, and that the big chief would be round to see him on Monday, at home.

Thank fuck, Dave thought. He would soon be out of this dry, non-smoking shithole. He would drink to that when the nurses' backs were turned, and he'd finished ogling them.

"Oh, and one more thing," said the copper, "this

will help you get your strength back". He took out a Pepperami, Dave's favourite snack. "I was in 'ere myself once after a bungled raid, so I know what it's like," he said with a wink, as he threw the contraband item to Dave. "Tell your mate what I told you."

And with that, the policeman was gone.

An hour or so later, Mick's relatives left, and it was just the trio again. Danny was glad to be back in the fold, but he was still wracked with guilt over leaving his friends to … Who knows what might have happened.

He walked over to Mick's bed and unscrewed the cap on his hip flask for him.

"I'm sorry, Mick," was all he could say.

"It's OK, buddy."

Realising that even lifting it would be a struggle for his wounded friend, Danny held the flask to Mick's lips (in a very manly way, of course, like when a soldier is injured in one of those black and white World War II films) and tilted it for him. He gave Mick a long pull on the brandy, and the Les Paul that Mick got for his 18th birthday quickly became the third best present he'd ever received (the blowjob he copped when he'd gone out to celebrate that night didn't get relegated quite so easily).

Danny walked over to the bed where his other roughed-up buddy was lying. Dave was equally grateful for his alcoholic apology and could have drained the whole bottle.

"I'm sorry, David."

"You're fine, mate," said Dave, decadently exhaling brandy fumes. "It's every man for himself out there." He said this with conviction, but he knew it was a lie – when you've got a man down, it's time for you to man up.

"You posh boys are never much use in a scrap anyway," said Dave.

"Pah!" said Danny. "Who spent their youth playing

football at their local comp, eh?"

Dave grinned at his friend's theorising and the gunning down he was about to receive.

"What is it they call it?" said Danny.

"Fuck off, posh boy," said Dave.

"The working-class ballet! Yes, that sounds about right, you mincing little *prole*. You leave boxing and rugger to us real men, okay? Yes, there's nothing like a muddy scrum to put hairs on your chest – you stick to your ballet."

Danny did a little mince which prompted a good deal of laughter from most of the men in the ward, who found great entertainment in the trio and their pluck and panache.

"Bollocks," said Dave. "The only fights you've had involved wet towels, drafty showers, and half-a-dozen giggling Harry Potters."

"Cunt," said Danny with a grin.

"Fucking posh ponce."

Mick was in stitches, and not just the ones above his eye from a broken beer bottle three nights earlier. They hurt like mad as his face stretched with laughter, but he didn't care. Normal service had been resumed, and that was all that mattered.

To an outsider, it may have seemed strange that Dave and Danny's exchange was friendly, but it was, without question. It was stranger still – perhaps – hearing fighting talk coming from an androgynous thesp like Danny, and this wasn't wasted on the dozen or so patients who were lapping this up.

"Well, chaps, it's been nice seeing you," said Danny, walking backwards and collecting the fedora he'd thrown on a nearby coat hanger on his way in before flipping it back on and patting it into place again. "But I must bid you farewell and wish you both a speedy recovery. No footsie after lights-out, now."

Chapter 16

If Dave was glad to be home, then he was doubly so to be out of the hospital, even though he wouldn't be breakdancing for a while.

Having been through an ordeal, he was comforted by the familiar smell of home as his crutches carried him over the threshold of his two-bedroomed street-corner house. Yes, at least fifty percent of it was stale cigarette smoke, but it was his stale cigarette smoke, and it welcomed and comforted him.

Dave had slept for most of the taxi ride back from the hospital. Getting in and out of the cab was bloody murder for Dave, and the cabbie blew his chances of a tip by not offering to help. Dave had had to do a bit of a balancing act as he put his key in the door – nothing new there, his detractors might say, but on this occasion his wobbling was caused by his shifting all of his weight onto one of his crutches. As he steered his key into the yellow Yale lock, he noticed the door was grimy, its old coat of lime-green paint now cracked and peeling. For some reason, this brought about an almost otherworldly melancholy in Dave that he wasn't able to shake off until he was inside, with the old green door shut firmly behind him.

Several letters were piled up on his doormat, but this didn't interest him enough to endure the agony of reaching down. Whatever it was could wait.

Dave was pleased to see that the house hadn't been entirely empty in his absence. His microphones, microphone stands and harmonicas were on his living room coffee table, having been returned by Mick's brothers Cliff and Jake, who had been good as gold in going back to The Sea Wall Inn to retrieve what was left of their equipment.

Yes, the Davies brothers were good men, and Dave would get them a drink as soon as he had the chance (even if they hadn't coiled his leads up in quite the way he liked).

As well as the stale cigarette smoke, Dave's vast record collection gave his house a timber-like, parcel paper odour – a bit like a library (which, if you thought about it, is exactly what it was). His spare bedroom could no longer contain his collection of blues, soul and jazz vinyl, so they were stacked along the left-hand side of the stairs (all neatly and alphabetically filed of course).

A good part of his living room was also dedicated to storing selected original $33\frac{1}{3}$ rpm vinyl discs, and if he'd had more space, he would have filled that too.

If you liked R&B, then there was almost certainly something here for you. There were some obvious choices, Chuck Berry, The Rolling Stones etc., but it was the connoisseur who was in for a treat: Little Walter, John Lee Hooker, T-Bone Walker, Charlie Musselwhite, Howlin' Wolf – they were all there. And if one of those student types who liked (or claimed to like) jazz showed up, they could amuse themselves with Cannonball Adderley, Miles Davis or Louis Armstrong, who were just the tip of the iceberg in a collection that went back to Jelly Roll Morton and Buddy Borden.

None of those modern 'experimentalists', though. Dave had long held a view that a junkie who tried to bring elements of 'avant-garde' into this great musical tradition was a pretentious charlatan or a bloody vandal. Either way, they could choke on their saxophones or their crack pipes as far as he was concerned.

He dropped his overnight bag in the hall and went through to the kitchen before he realised he'd forgotten the golden rule: always buy a pint of milk on the journey home. No matter how far you've travelled or how long you've been away you must do this. Even if you've been to sea (or, in Dave's case, The Sea Wall Inn), the homecoming ritual wasn't the same if you couldn't put the kettle on and make a cuppa.

Forget this, and you were left with two choices. Either you could sit back in your favourite chair, switch on the TV and bask in the comforts of home without a fresh brew, which was just wrong, or you could put your coat back on and leave your place of safety and go and brave the elements once again. Neither had much appeal, for either way the magic was gone. Or it would be if Dave didn't have another plan up his sleeve/in his fridge: Budweiser beer. After all, a beer *was* a brew – to an American, anyway.

This was all the reasoning it took. Well, this and the fact that Dave liked cold beer more than hot tea (and probably more than he should, he was starting to suspect).

But he'd been through an ordeal, and this was a good enough excuse. He fetched a brew and hobbled back to the living room, sitting down on his two-seat beige couch in the spot where he'd recently noticed his own groove was forming.

As well as being comforted by the smell of his house, his couch had reassuring qualities of its own. It came from the living room of the Hunter family home back in Southend-on-Sea. His late father had brought the smell of curing cement home with him, and over the years this buried itself in the stitches and fabric of the sofa, and it was still there however faintly to that day.

As a lad, Dave often spent Sunday mornings climbing trees and playing football, just the usual boys' larks, and his mum would yell at him for coming home covered in mud. He'd be told to get in the bath then change his clothes, then after one of Mum's Sunday roasts he would doze for most of the afternoon on the couch he now had in his own living room. To this day he would sometimes drift off and wake up thinking he could smell beef dripping, half expecting to hear his mum calling him for his tea.

Dave kept his weakness for nostalgia under control.

He knew enough alcoholics to know the danger of living in what Stevie Wonder had called a 'pastime paradise', but that didn't stop him enjoying the occasional stroll down memory lane.

He forgot to switch the TV on before he sat down (once he was comfy he did not intend to get up again for a long, long time) but his stereo was in within reach of the couch on a small wooden table beside it. He still hadn't played the flip side of the mysterious vinyl, and he decided this was the perfect opportunity. He was home and dry in his favourite sitting/listening position. He had blues, he had a beer, and he had seventeen Benson and Hedges cigarettes: time to mellow down easy and forget all about his recent near-death experience.

He flipped the vinyl and cracked his Bud open in that order. Then he sat back, closed his eyes and put his first beer in a long time to his lips. But if he expected to relax, he'd be disappointed.

He'd barely taken a chug of his cold Bud when the music started, and much like Mick did with that roughneck in Thurrock, it grabbed him by the balls.

Unlike the first side of the album, side two (an alien concept to today's so-called music lovers) was a studio recording and a damn sight better for it. The first song started with an acoustic guitar that was joined by a tambourine around the time the voice came in. Or around the time the voice roared up, rather.

Whoever Bobby Fulton was, Dave heard straight away that he was phenomenal. Soulful and expressive, this guy had it all. His voice was raw and throaty, like a young Frankie Miller or Rod Stewart, only with more bass. It was a voice that came from the heart and from the gut, and he had perfect pitch too. Yes, this guy was from the Thames Delta and not the more celebrated Mississippi one, but Dave could barely hear the difference.

Track one was a quick rip through *I Heard it*

Through the Grapevine which not only overcame the lack of a rhythm section but was enhanced by the simple guitar-and-voice format.

Next up was a tough stomp through *Rollin and Tumblin*, sung with so much fire that Dave thought his speakers might catch alight. About halfway through, some slide guitar got underway, and the guitarist (was Fulton on guitar?) stomped his foot to make up for the lack of a drummer, but he needn't have bothered.

Dave felt his cigarette burn his fingers: he'd become so engrossed in the music he'd forgotten all about the 'growler' he'd lit a moment ago. He found a space for it in his ashtray along with about forty others and lit another one. He forgot to smoke this one as well, lost in the music as he was.

Then there was a knock on the door, and Dave cursed his visitor's timing.

Chapter 17

The knock at the door was a policeman's knock, and this wasn't just any policeman.

Ted Maskell ('The Sarge'), 57

Sergeant Ted Maskell of Essex Police and attached to Thurrock Police Station was a lifelong friend of Dave's as was any friend of his late father.

Like Dave, The Sarge was a music enthusiast with a love of blues and blues harmonica. He taught Dave almost everything he knew, and although he was no professional, and he had been overtaken by his ex-student, Maskell kept his chops up and maintained his interest. A police officer of twenty-nine years, Maskell had seen all there was to see and took pride in his work.

Once Dave had endured the agony of getting up to answer the door, he showed his friend in and reclaimed his favourite spot on the couch.

"Get me one an' all," he called out to Maskell, who clearly planned to visit the kitchen fridge before he did any talking.

"Blimey," said The Sarge when he came back to the living room with a cold beer in either hand. "Those big boys play rough, don't they?"

"Well, Sarge, I won't be doing the chicken or the mashed potato for a while, let's put it that way."

For a moment there was silence.

"You won't be surprised to learn that we've not shed any light on the identity of your attacker," said Maskell with an air of disappointment by way of an apology. "Always the way, I'm afraid. Their lot has a strict code about talking to authority figures, and us coppers are the worst o' the lot as far as they're concerned. As for your homesteaders, well, they're even less likely to talk to us for fear of reprisal." He shook his head at this pitiful state of affairs.

"Do you know," he said, looking Dave right in the eye, "I told the landlord of The Sea Wall Inn he ought to throw his pool table out and get a pinball machine for all those deaf, dumb and blind customers of his."

"Ah yes," said Dave, "the landlord. What did he have to say?"

"Apparently they – whoever *they* are – paid for the booking in cash and didn't leave a name, address or a phone number. Seems fishy if you ask me."

The Sarge took a sip of his beer, and for a moment he seemed lost in deepest thought.

"Mind you," he said eventually, " I can't say I blame him for wanting to keep schtum. The last thing a publican wants is for his pub to burn down – not while he's in the black, anyway."

Another silence followed. It was hard for The Sarge to know what to say to someone who was in great pain, who had just got out of hospital and when he was only telling him what he expected to hear.

Dave, on the other hand, didn't feel like talking much about anything even though the Sergeant was a good friend of his.

"Anyway, I hope you won't be resting up for too long," said The Sarge encouragingly. "Your Dad was proud of you and rightly so – you can't let a little thing like this hold you back."

"Don't be daft, Sarge. You can't keep a good man down – you know that, right?"

The Sarge didn't need to answer. He just raised an eyebrow in agreement while taking another pull on his Bud.

Dave wasn't referring to a particular incident here, but it was no secret that The Sarge could handle himself and could get stuck in when he had to. After all, you couldn't pound the beat in the toughest county in England without getting a bruise or a blister.

"Tell me, Sarge, have you ever heard of this lot?" said Dave as he held up the sleeve of the record that was on his deck right now, spinning away with the volume turned down.

Maskell looked at the front cover for a second then shook his head, but only after a quick double-take.

"Doesn't ring any bells, I'm afraid."

Dave thought this was a fair answer, or at least it would have been if he'd believed him. Which he didn't.

"I guess it was a long shot," said Dave, not particularly convinced.

"I've seen so many bands in my time," said The Sarge.

This was true. The Sarge had followed dozens of bands through the years, and he'd even roadied for some of them. He'd also been to see Dave play many times and still did now and again, work and Masonic duties permitting.

But the first bit wasn't true, and Dave was sure of it.

It wasn't long before the Sergeant's visit was over. He told Dave he would require a statement in due course, thanked him for the beer and in return was thanked for the Pepperami and saw himself out.

Dave thought there was something strange about all of this. Ted Maskell was a big man who had faced danger all his life, doing what was right without fear or favour. Yet one glance at the record cover of some forgotten Essex bluesman, and it was like someone had walked over his grave. He'd done a better-than-average job of masking his surprise, but it was there alright – Dave could see it in his eyes.

And he didn't like it one little bit.

It wasn't just surprise that Dave saw on the face of The Sarge; it was fear. It troubled Dave to see this in a man that he had looked up to as a boy, but it puzzled him as well.

Worst of all was the fact that his friend had lied to

him. Dave could live with being lied to by a copper, but being lied to by a friend? That was another matter, and it required his immediate attention.

For some time, Dave had been curious about the man whose voice was buried in those wax grooves, what his story was, where he was now, etc. He wanted to find out everything there was to know about Bobby Fulton, and he was bloody well going to an' all.

Time marched on until Dave saw a street light flick on outside his living room window, and he realised he was sitting in darkness save for the light from his cigarette and the ghostly glow from his stereo's display panel.

While Dave was with Sergeant Maskell, Danny was in his flat nursing a brandy with the lights down.

It was a good brandy taken from the same bottle he'd topped his friends' flasks up with the other day. Danny usually enjoyed this beverage, and its exquisite taste and high alcohol content should have put him in a celebratory mood. But tonight Danny wasn't feeling it – 'it' being the high spirits that came from drinking expensive brandy, pilfered from his father's drinks cabinet while visiting the family home over Christmas.

He was feeling something though: guilt. He had left his friends for dead.

Sure, they all laughed about it at the hospital the other day, and there'd been no ill-feeling from either of them. This should have been the end of it, but it wasn't for Danny.

Since that night, Danny had found himself avoiding his own stare in the mirror every time he tried to comb that floppy, girly hair of his. Going on campus didn't seem right while his friends were too gammy to follow suit, and worst of all he'd stopped following the teachings of his beloved Jools Holland: he didn't start each day with a boogie, he started each day with a *brandy*. He knew where all this guilt and shame came from (his privileged upbringing, mainly), but this didn't make him feel better or anything like a man again.

There was a long tradition of men in the Blyth family doing military service. His father did several tours of Northern Ireland before he joined the family shipping business, and *his* father had fought in the second world war. Danny had an older brother who had just come back from Iraq, and it had never been hard to see which of the two brothers the family were proudest of.

Until recently this had bothered him, but now he could see why. His brother had courage and loyalty, two things he had hardly demonstrated the other night when it all got a bit hairy and his friends were wounded, he reminded himself bitterly.

It wasn't just his brother with whom these unflattering comparisons were drawn – his younger sister Violet had recently muscled in as well. She was a fully

171

paid-up member of the public sector, something their father spoke of with enormous pride. Danny suspected her role wasn't as glamorous or as important as their father's squiffy boasts suggested ('my daughter works in government, don't you know'), but it wasn't like Danny had been asked to play the piano for guests over the recent festive period.

The brandy was doing little to lighten his mood, but he sipped at it anyway. If my friends could see me now, he thought.

They'd probably think even less of you, posh boy.

After a while, he got up from his chair and walked his healthy, able body over to the window and looked out across the darkening skyline. This isn't over, he thought. Not by a long shot. Danny had Dave and Mick's friendship, but he needed to have their respect.

He would get it back by any means possible.

Chapter 18

One of the best things about living in the toughest county in England was that you could walk into a pub with a black eye and a plaster cast and no-one would look up from their pint. Wonky conk? Seen it all before, mate. Throttle marks? Pah! It takes more than that to get any sympathy out of this hardy bunch.

Dave wondered if it had been like this in ye olden times. Had people once gone into hostelries such as The Hole in the Wall, or The Castle on what was now the high street with musket wounds or spears in their sides, only to have the barmaid tell them the Carling's off and they'd have to drink bottled lager instead? Knowing this lot, Dave imagined the answer was probably yes.

In Essex, having the shit beaten out of you was seen as a rite of passage and you were considered green and virginal until you had experienced this. That's why Essex menfolk played this kind of thing down, and so did some of the women.

There was always one though, and it was usually the same one. Tonight, as usual, it was the turn of the barman in the green shirt and green tie. As soon as Dave had downed his chaser there came the expected "careful – you'll be *legless*," but if Dennis wanted to get a laugh out of this, then he'd be disappointed.

The Red Lion's landlord wasn't the only one who had noticed Dave's injuries. On the way in, Dave passed two local old boys, out past their bedtime playing arthritic dominoes. As they struggled to remember whose go it was, they talked about the old times, sharing fond recollections of blackouts, rationing and living in abject poverty.

"Looks like that young man's been set upon," said one of the old boys.

"Ahh," sighed the other one wearily. "There was never any violence in our day – not during the war."

Walking the quarter of a mile from his house to The Red Lion had taken Dave much longer than usual. Luckily, there was an empty barstool where he could sit and rest his bones, broken or otherwise, and sup his pint. The chaser took effect, and the world became a little bit more cheerful. Dave heard music in the incessant beeping of the fruit machines and the jangly payouts they sometimes made, and he heard life in the raspy laughter of the middle-aged 'sorts' in the taproom.

"Oi Barney!" said Dave, calling out to one of the regulars who was standing three feet away from him but who was at least two-thirds 'mutton'. He gave the dumpy middle-aged man with a veiny face and a prune for a nose a few pound coins and pointed towards the jukebox, not needing to explain why he couldn't really do it for himself.

"Something good, eh?"

Dave knew there'd be no Bobby Bland or Chris Farlowe on the jukebox, but there might be some Rod

Stewart, and that would do for now.

Barney was an odd character. He didn't talk much, and the only subject he warmed to was dogs. Dogs, and his total lack of fear of them, that was. Barney claimed he wasn't scared of any dog in the world and reckoned he knew exactly how to defend himself in an attack. Some people found this to be a strange thing to discuss in a social setting, and it probably was better suited to an army barracks, a prison or another form of secure unit. But, Dave liked to give people the time of day no matter how mad they seemed, and he only sometimes smiled at himself as he did so.

In fact, Dave had started to wonder recently if polite society's squeamishness and perceived social norms could be their downfall. Would the average citizen know how to fend off an attack from an Alsatian or a Rottweiler? Dave did, and while it wasn't pretty (it really, really wasn't), he knew it could come in handy one day. Barney also talked about darts sometimes, and even for Dave, this was a bridge too far.

It saddened Dave to hear Barney recall his glory days of winning the Colchester East Region Darts League final for the third year in a row, twenty years ago. Barney was forty, but he looked fifteen years older, and it was hard for Dave not to feel sorry for someone whose life had passed him by in a haze of pub banter, darts scores and catching last orders. Barney seemed happy with his lot, but if anything this made it worse (Dave was aware of the fact that he risked going the same way).

This unpleasant thought was blasted away by the pub's trusty speakers, which came roaring to life to the strains of Rod the Mod's excellent cover of Chuck's *Sweet Little Rock 'n' Roller* (nice one, Barney!). This cheered Dave up as good music always did. The mood in the room seemed to lift a little too, despite it being a quiet Monday night.

It was also quiet outside Leggero's, down in Thurrock, where 'Left-Handed' Pete and Slouch were needlessly keeping watch. There were a few drunks and vagrants here, a couple of angry-looking Irishmen there, a few businessmen ripped to the gills on champagne that was sold expensively but bought cheaply, talking loudly about take-overs to anyone who would listen – there'd be no trouble tonight.

In fact, there was something depressingly familiar about it – especially for Slouch, who had seen this a thousand times before. The drunks would drink until they could do so no more or until they were told it was time to go. Which was fine for the ones who had homes to go to, and even Slouch or Pete could feel sorry for a man with nowhere to go on a night like this.

Before long, the talk among the businessmen would turn from mergers and takeovers to cocaine and hookers. They would make their way separately into the night, perhaps 'hunting honey with money to burn', as Elton John once sang but more likely in search of somewhere quiet to go and have a little cry. The other stragglers would soon follow, then the DJ would finish his set before midnight and sneak off for some shut-eye (he had school in the morning). It was dull, it was routine, and it was boring.

This was bad news for Slouch and Pete since boredom is the worst thing in the world when you have a lot on your mind. Boredom breeds restlessness in the minds of troubled souls and leads to tension and paranoia. All of the bad stuff comes to the fore when a man is left alone with just time and his thoughts.

And being left alone with their time and their thoughts is exactly what would happen to them if this Kent job went wrong. The indignity of a man in his fifty-eighth year having to use communal showers thought 'Left-handed' Pete. He actually found himself hoping someone would start some trouble just to give him something to take his mind off it.

Slouch, on the other hand, had something to distract him from their mission, but it was related to it, and it was something quite horrible.

That morning he had been for a consultation with the private surgeon who would be in charge of removing his 'inks' via a series of dermabrasions. Slouch hadn't liked the sound of this, and he had been right not to. Dermabrasion, he'd learned, was essentially the practice of carving and mutilating the skin – in his case to get rid of his tattoos. The surgeon had smiled as he'd explained the symptoms which, as Slouch had suspected, were very bad indeed. They would be painful and long-lasting, and that wasn't all.

The doctor told Slouch there was also 'risk of infection leading to sores on the body and face of the patient'. Pete had been quick to point out that he got enough of these from the girls he sometimes goes to see, but it hadn't made him feel any better.

Not for the first time in the last two weeks, Slouch began to wonder if his life would have been less painful and a lot safer if they'd just let him stay in the army.

Chapter 19

There was something heroic about the way Dave made it back from the pub last night. Six pints with chasers was going some for an able-bodied customer, let alone a man in a state of disrepair.

For practical reasons, he'd declined the landlord's offer of a lift. However difficult it was to stay vertical in his condition, it was easier and less painful than getting in and out of a car. Dave was getting the hang of his crutches now, so he fancied the practise.

There was also the small matter of Dennis matching Dave pint for a pint and short for short the whole time he'd been there.

Once he was home and dry, Dave took his favourite place on the couch and gave his new favourite LP another spin over a lovely Jameson. He enjoyed losing himself in those deep grooves and booze fumes, but then came sleepiness, which seemed strange as he'd been unconscious for much of the last week.

Before he dozed off, he inspected the back cover of the LP. It had the customary black and white stage door photo, with the band and what he'd first assumed were hangers-on but on closer inspection decided must have been roadies on account of their demeanour and the way their knuckles hung.

It turned out the album had been recorded (but perhaps not released) in 1979, and the reverse side of the sleeve also bore the logo of 'Matchbox Music Co' in the bottom left corner. The logo was simple but effective. It was basically the company's name inside a small yellow box with a vinyl disc instead of the 'o' in 'Matchbox' and a matchstick in place of the 'i' in 'Music'. Underneath the logo, the company name was drawn in the form of a signature with a burning match for a pen, the way children tried to write their names with sparklers on bonfire night.

Dave found it strange that he'd not heard of this record label and wondered if he could find out more about it on that thing that everyone on campus was talking about. What was it? On your computer – that 'net' thing?

He didn't like the sound of that (and by this time the booze was kicking in hard), but just as his eyes began to close he remembered Danny saying he had a sister. What was her name? Rose, perhaps? Hadn't Danny said something about her working in the city? Ah yes, Dave thought as he settled down for the night, not feeling much like climbing the stairs. He'd get up early and call Danny first thing and have him look into it.

It was 11:30 am, and the getting up early part of Dave's plan had been well and truly blown out of the water. He was hungover and aching from head to foot, but he would call Danny nonetheless. He forced himself to sit upright and reached for the phone, neither of which was easy. He lifted the receiver and keyed in Danny's landline number from memory. After half a dozen rings Danny picked up, sounding like he'd started early.

"David! Darling!"

It really was hard to tell with him.

"Yes, hello Danny," said Dave, wondering why Daniel Blyth answered the phone like this every time he called him.

"How is one? And how are things in the dangerous and exciting world of our county's finest sparring son? Tell me, are we going to go back there and find the little urchin are we? Eh? What's say we stiffen the sinews and summon up the blood and give this rascal a fucking good hiding? I'm game if you are."

"Well, Danny, I'm a bit of a raspberry at the moment so it might have to wait. Listen, I need a favour. You said something about your sister a little while back – what's her name? Violet or something?"

"The very same. I've heard she's been making a bit

of a name for herself in the city as a party girl. Oh, *why* can't she find herself a nice young man and settle d –"

"Not now, Danny," said Dave. "Where does she work, and what does she do there?"

"Well, our father would have you believe otherwise, but in fact, she's a lowly office junior at Companies House."

You fucking *beauty.*

"Danny, I love you."

"Why, I'm rather fond of you t –"

"Shut up. Now, you said she was a crafty one, right? Give her a call and have her run a search or whatever they call it on Matchbox Records. Tell her that anything she can find will help me."

"Consider it done. Toodle pip."

I'll toodle pip you, posh boy, thought Dave as the receiver went dead.

"If they catch me here I'm fucking dead," said the runner, seeing his breath in the cold morning air.

Like anyone who had seen day turn to night then back again, his mood had darkened – but his grim prediction was no fantasy. He would face death if 'they' knew he was here, and the knowledge that it would probably be over quickly offered him little comfort.

'They', in this instance were the two brothers at the top table of the Cleaver gang; 'here' was the long and winding private road that led to the house of Norman Layer, a man even more feared than his 'bosses'.

The man in the running shoes wasn't spending Monday morning sleeping off the whisky from the poker game the night before like his colleagues were. Instead, he was risking his life reporting to his real paymaster to share information about his assumed ones. He'd been doing this every Monday morning for the last three months, and privately, he wondered how much longer his body could cope with the mix of booze, adrenaline and nervous exhaustion.

There wasn't much for him to report today – just a few scraps of information that could help with the planning of the upcoming job in Kent. The important details – the who's, what's and where's and the weapons that the Cleavers' men would be carrying – were already known and had been worked into the plan several weeks earlier. He was really only there because the boss wanted him there, and when the boss said jump, you jumped.

This lowly courier had a name, and it carried weight in both of the organisations he worked for.

Phillip Howlens, 29

Howlens was a 'brain', even though it was hard for him to feel like one running through the streets like a messenger of old with just his tracksuit, his baseball cap and a disguising hood to connect him to the modern era.

It was his brains that had got him an 'in' with Norman Layer – that, and the fact that his father had done time for him. Howlens hadn't had an easy ride, but he was certainly of value to the company. He was quick-thinking, fast on his feet, and most importantly, he was an excellent liar. Norman Layer was good at spotting a liar, and it was a skill he valued enormously; to him, it showed potential.

Howlens had been head-hunted by the Cleaver brothers five years earlier. Or more precisely, he'd engineered a game of cat and mouse that led to the two brothers hiring him, thinking he was onside.

He allowed himself to be caught selling cocaine in one of their London nightclubs. He was apprehended and taken upstairs, where he withstood an interrogation from two of the Cleavers' 'heavies', refusing to provide even the basic name, rank and file details that captured soldiers are obliged to give. Howlens was searched thoroughly, and while his captors didn't find the hairpin he'd bent to shape around his bottom row of teeth, they did find a book of matches from a Soho nightspot in the breast pocket of his suit.

Eventually, the heavies took a break from the interrogation, and Howlens was left handcuffed to a radiator in the boardroom where his grilling had just taken place. The secret pin made it easy for him to lose the handcuffs and soon he was off, down the drainpipe and away like a thief in the night

The matchbook was a plant, and all Howlens had to do was frequent the nightclub it came from until he was sent for. Which he was, two days later. He could have been killed there and then, but the Cleavers thought he could be useful to them alive.

Howlens was nicknamed 'Kamikaze Joe' within the Cleaver gang due to his almost suicidal willingness to sell drugs on rival turfs. This brought him into contact with lots of angry dealers who would demand to know who he worked for. They found out, of course, but by then it was too late. The small-time pushers and pimps that Howlens brought out of the shadows in this way were beaten and threatened with guns and knives, before being relieved of their product and ultimately put out of business. It was an effective process that after a dozen or so repeats had allowed the Cleaver brothers to monopolise London's lucrative drugs market.

Which like little lambs to the slaughter, they now stood to lose all in one night, thanks to their trusted aide, Mr Phillip Howlens.

This had earned him great praise from his father's old mate, Norman Layer, who rewarded this young man's derring-do with a lifestyle he could only have dreamt of had he put his espionage skills to use legally. Howlens had a trophy wife, a sports car, a swanky Kensington flat, plus membership of any number of exclusive London members' clubs, which he would have visited more often if only the conversation went beyond house prices and school fees.

Howlens was younger than most of the men in Layer's organisation, and though he'd never admit it, people like Slouch, Shark etc. scared him a bit, made him uneasy. Howlens was no 'bottle job', but there was something primal, something savage about these men that troubled him.

He thought this might be a generational thing. These were men who as boys had been taught boxing at school and spent their Saturdays climbing around bombed-out buildings while their parents drank, haunted by memories of the war that had created the wreckage their children now played in. As these boys became young men, many of them were called up for National Service, and several stayed on to become fully paid-up soldiers. In part they did this to make a better life for themselves; mostly, however, they did it to find an outlet for their aggression and perhaps shoot a few foreigners while they were at it.

Might pull a few birds, too.

Howlens had a stitch from all the running. Only half a mile to go, he thought as he caught his breath in the cold air. He'd be glad when this was all over.

Chapter 20

It was April and the days were getting longer and warmer. Dave had a new spring in his step, for not only had spring now sprung, but his cast was off, his leg was healed, and his crutches had long since been chucked in a skip near the end of his street.

Soon, he would be playing football again, and if he wasn't up to Gary Lineker standard by the time of his first five-a-side match, then he could find comfort in the fact that he'd been none too clever in the first place.

Better still, Danny, Mick and Dave had been asked to play at the famous Colne Blues Festival in the summer. That was always a good day out, and Dave was thinking about hiring a coach and taking some of his mates from The Red Lion for a beano.

Yes, these were good times indeed for Dave and the gang, who had been keeping their chops up with their

Monday night 'unplugged' sessions at Dave's place, as well as attending a weekly open-mic night at a pub in nearby Wivenhoe every Wednesday.

The hardest part of the open mic night was getting a slot to perform. That or sitting through the poetry readings, much of which to Dave's ears was worse than the Vogon torture poetry in the *Hitchhiker's Guide* series. But it was house policy that everyone got a turn, even though Dave thought it was wrong to encourage them.

There were also several middle-aged or upwards singer-songwriter types – crusty old Bob Dylan/Leonard Cohen wannabes usually – but they could be dealt with quickly enough. Light heckling often did the job, and although Dave recognised one or two of them as lecturers from the university, it did little to stop him.

Danny had asked Dave why he insisted that they went to these things. Dave, being the oldest and the wisest of the three, explained to Danny that it was important to keep playing while they were off the road because musicians got rusty quicker than they improved. He didn't half ask some questions, Dave had thought at the time, but he'd learn, bless him.

Mick, on the other hand, went along with it, which Dave took as a good sign. As for Nicky and Ricky, the spineless rhythm section last seen hot-footing it back from Thurrock, well, they'd be contacted when the time was right and not shot for desertion as Mick had suggested.

Mick and Danny had also become enamoured with the mysterious 12-inch $33\frac{1}{3}$ rpm wax cylinder that was slowly being worn out on Dave's turntable; newcomers though they were, these two knew chops when they heard them – another good sign.

Oddly enough, though, Dave had lost interest in finding this Fulton chap. He'd found out through Danny's sister that Matchbox Records was formed in 1978 by a Mr Norman Layer and had ceased trading in 1980. Other than that and the fact that the company had held a London PO Box, this was the only information available. Dave had jotted this down on the reporter's notebook he kept by his phone, but he had done it half-heartedly with little in the way of expectation.

This, of course, was about to change.

It was Monday night, and Dave was getting ready for a jam session. He'd bought enough beer to quench an army's thirst, a bottle of 'Jack', and several bags of salty snacks. He'd even had his third tidy-up of the year, knowing that a fourth would be in order once this lot was finished.

He was just packing away the last of the breakables when he heard a knock at the door, which was strange since it was only seven-thirty and Danny and Mick weren't due for another half-hour.

To Dave's pleasant surprise, it was his old pal Ted Maskell – The Sarge.

"Blimey," said Dave. "Did you get a transfer?"

"Force guidelines suggest all officers take a different route to and from work every day," said Maskell with a wink. "I'm also thinking about moving out this way – I've heard it's safer round here."

"You might well be right, me old china plate. Come on in," said Dave as he gestured for his friend to come inside.

Maskell couldn't help but notice how tidy the place was for a change.

"I 'ope I'm not intruding," he said, actually meaning *'I can piss off if you've got a bird coming round.'*

"You're fine, mate. The boys are coming over for a jam later," was the response he had hoped for and the one he got, and to his delight, Dave asked him to stay and join in.

The good sergeant must have had a sixth sense, for he opened his jacket and showed Dave a belt underneath it with holders for all twelve of his harmonicas. The Sarge grinned, and he knew that Dave knew that he'd had this planned all along.

Ted Maskell was a terrific musician, albeit one who sadly lacked the confidence to play in public. Danny and Mick arrived soon after Maskell, and the three of them blew up a storm on some old blues tunes. With Mick on acoustic guitar and Danny playing a crappy little Casio keyboard (Dave had taught them long ago that necessity is the mother of invention) and Sarge on harmonica, they played with gusto and feeling. Each song provided a springboard for some inspired, purposeful improvisation, and every player got the chance to stretch out a bit.

Dave acted simply as bartender and host to this makeshift power trio, and it was all he needed to do. Much like his hero and fellow bandleader Muddy Waters, Dave Hunter came from a culture of jamming, and he liked to give everyone a chance to shine and see where the song took them. He never played over someone else's solo, and he didn't let his solos outstay their welcome either.

The thing was, he hadn't had to learn this from any of his various mentors over the years. He'd listened to them, listened to everything they said in fact. But he hadn't needed to; he just 'got it'.

This was why Dave Hunter led where others followed; he knew things that couldn't be taught.

One thing he knew only too well was that musicians who played too many notes or relied on excessive volume usually did so because they were arrogant or insecure, and Dave Hunter was neither. Well, maybe a touch the former, but his ego was firmly in check, and his approach had served him well.

Two hours passed in a haze of merriment before Dave called for a break, and each of the men filled their glasses. It had been a blast, and the good vibe remained – until The Sarge asked if he could use Dave's phone, that was.

As he lifted the receiver, Sarge clocked the name that Dave had scribbled on the pad next to his phone several weeks earlier. Dave noticed The Sarge had turned pale, like he'd given blood and seen a ghost the same day. It was the same haunted expression Dave had seen the day he got out of the hospital, and he'd shown Sarge the mystery vinyl.

"Listen, boys, I'm on a long early tomorrow – I'd best be on my way," said The Sarge. "Thanks for everything, mind – let's do it again sometime, eh?"

He put his jacket on and walked towards the door with Dave not far behind him to see him out. Once he was over the threshold, The Sarge paused but didn't look back. Instead, he fixed his gaze on the dark empty street outside.

"Sarge, are you alright, mate?" said Dave. "I'm not gonna lie, you've got me a bit spooked here."

Still, the sergeant faced the night, and it seemed

strange for one so confident not to make eye contact. After a lengthy silence, he turned and faced his friend once more.

"Mind how you go," he said. "Look after yourself, yeah?"

Then he was gone, and never in Dave's life had a throwaway parting line sounded so loaded.

Back in Dave's living room, it was left to the three musketeers to mull over what it was that had rattled this hard man (The Sarge was definitely that).

Not in the mood for more playing, they set their instruments down and drank and smoked and talked and ... They didn't seem to be getting anywhere. But the fact that Danny, who didn't have the best interpersonal skills in the world had picked up on Maskell's dark vibes only added to the suspicion that strange and possibly very bad things were afoot in the Essex delta.

"Tell you what, I'll call my sister in the morning and see if she's got any more leads on Matchbox Records or this Norman Layer chap," said Danny.

"No," said Dave. "Not yet, anyway."

He turned to Danny to explain his decision.

"We mustn't play all of our cards at once. We've got to keep something in reserve. Whoever or whatever this is has got 'Deputy Dawg' scared, so it doesn't seem right to involve your sister, does it?"

Danny nodded in agreement, unaware that Dave's real thought process went something like this: *given the nature of the job and the possibility of danger, your army-trained brother might be more useful than your little sister Violet.*

Dave sat in his favourite sofa space and once more perused the back cover of the record that had somehow spooked his policeman friend.

"This is all very exciting," said Mick, "but don't you think you're getting a bit carried away here?"

"He's right," said Danny. "We're never going to

solve the mystery, are we?" he said, perhaps more as a statement than a question.

Then Dave burst to his feet like Sherlock Holmes and the deal was done.

"Oh yes, we are," he said. "Oh yes, we are!" This was followed by a long, loud laugh that made the others nervous.

"What is it?" asked Mick, which earned him no more than a '*not now, you'll have to wait, but I've got something good up my sleeve*'-style finger-wagging from Dave.

"Gentlemen," said Dave. "Rest ye now, for we meet at dawn."

"Dawn?" asked Mick, not convinced.

"Okay, nine-thirty going on ten," he said, ditching the theatrics but keeping his beaming smile.

"What are you up to, old boy?" said Danny with a mischievous grin.

"We'll start with a nice full English to build our strength up," said Dave. "Then, we're gonna jump in the old Subaru Impreza, fire her up, and that, gentlemen, is where the adventure will begin."

Mick was suspicious. "Building up strength? Adventure? Getting in a car? With you driving? Dave … What's going on?"

He shook his head, but Dave nodded with such vigour that Mick knew right away he'd lost and that resistance was useless. Then Dave said it.

"We're going back to Thurrock."

Chapter 21

At around eleven the following morning, an unusually fresh-faced Dave answered the door to a distinctly rough-looking Danny and Mick. It turned out the two of them had been drinking for much of the two-mile walk back to Danny's last night then carried on when they got there.

"Get inside," said Dave. "I've got just the thing."

'Just the thing' turned out to be Dave's patented hangover busting concoction. It was a banana smoothie with lime juice, tomato juice and two dissolved aspirins. And two crunched-up Vitamin B tablets. And a shot of Lucozade (the only shots they'd be drinking for a while). There was also Red Bull, a sip of orange juice, a trickle of Tabasco, Worcester sauce and some Dr Pepper (Dave put Dr Pepper in because it tasted nasty, and this was supposed to be a punishment after all).

The ingredients were mixed together in a pint glass

and had to be taken down in one gulp by the patient, as they rarely managed a second. Its taste, Dave had been informed since he'd never drunk one himself, was truly revolting; but if the victim kept it down, they would be on their way towards a quick and full recovery. And if they didn't, likewise, for it was just the clean-out their poor systems needed.

Dave had mixed these in advance having guessed this would happen, and he led his disgraced friends out to the back garden to start their recovery ritual.

Through gritted teeth, Mick got down to the bottom of his glass in a record six seconds. Not many had done it that quickly, and Dave was impressed. Danny fared less well and only made it three-quarters of the way down before being violently sick in Dave's neglected vegetable patch.

Danny and Mick stood there for a moment, relieved that it was over but aghast at the horror they had endured.

Soon, however, they both felt as if they had been touched by the hand of God such was the miracle of their recovery. Dave saw the colour coming back to Danny's cheeks, and Mick was starting to look more alive by the second; he decided they were ready for work.

"And now, gentlemen," he said. "A hearty feast before we ride into battle."

As they tucked into a full English breakfast, Dave told them what it was he saw last night that had made the light bulb appear above his head. The back cover of the record showed a picture of Bobby Fulton and his band outside the backstage loading area of a venue Dave was prepared to wager was Hammersmith Odeon or whatever it was called these days. A small army of crew members was lingering in the background, along with an assortment of female fans perhaps seeking notoriety in the groupie community.

What had made Dave jump out of his seat last night

was a moment of snap recognition (he had a photographic memory albeit one that sometimes took a bit longer to process images than your local Boots developing counter). Dave had seen one of the roadies in the picture before – he just couldn't say where or when.

Until the answer came to him out of the blue last night, that was. As he'd perused the record's front and back covers, Dave had subconsciously cast his mind back to the night in January that had nearly cost him and his friends their lives.

As they'd tried to find the venue that night, they passed a restaurant-cum-bar-cum-nightclub opposite the section of the seawall that faces Grays' town centre. Dave didn't remember the name of the place, but he did remember the face of one its doormen. It belonged to a tough-looking chap with a shaved head and attitude to burn.

A younger version of which lurked on the flip side of the LP Dave was holding last night. In the picture, the man was lurking in the background, at home in the shadows, but it was him alright.

***

"Are you sure about this?" said Danny, leaning forward from the backseat of Dave's Subaru, that was trundling up the slip road onto the Southbound A12.

"One hundred percent, Danny. One-hundred percent."

"He didn't look familiar to me – I was there too," said Danny.

"Me neither," said Mick, chipping in.

"That's because you were trying to read street names in hazardous conditions, Mickey-boy. Danny was pie-eyed as ever so that just leaves me to take in the scenery. And trust me, boys, it's him."

"OK, so what if this bloke you saw outside the nightclub is the man in the photograph?" said Mick. "What are we gonna do? Make a citizen's arrest?"

"Don't think I haven't thought about it," said Dave. "Never say never right?"

No answer came, so he continued. "No, I'm not saying we nick him. That's Sergeant Maskell's job – unless he's too scared, poor old bugger.

"Come on, boys, use your imagination. We just need to do some digging. Follow this bloke around a bit, see who he works for – that kind of thing. We need to get a feel for the place. We're all musicians, so let's improvise. Come on – where's your sense of adventure?"

"Hey – we could steal his phone or his wallet," said Danny. "Better still, we could follow him home, wait 'til he goes out again, break in and have a little look-see around his house."

"Now you're talking. Very good, Daniel-san," Dave said with a smile, pleased that at least one of his sidekicks was along for the ride.

It had been a long time since something had got

Dave switched on like this, and he was enjoying it enormously. Whether he was enjoying it in spite of the potential threat to his well-being or simply because of it, he couldn't be sure, but he was in his element after the rot that had set in well before his beating at the hands of a psychotic Irishman.

Was his gloom a product of post-Christmas depression, or 'Blue Monday' as some people called it? Was it the fact that a cocky American had taken an interest in the same girl that he had had his eyes on, and his growing sense that the battle was being lost?

It had occurred to Dave recently that his downward trajectory could be traced back to the first time he ever laid eyes on her. He remembered a feeling that something was wrong that day despite his instant enamour; a disquiet came over him that didn't quite fade away into the laughter and the ambience of the taproom that night.

"Listen," said Dave. "All we're doing is a bit of

research – same as we would if we were at uni. The only difference is that we might find out something useful, get our hands dirty, feel our pulses quicken perhaps. And we won't get that from a quiet afternoon in the library looking for a way to tell some silly old professor something he already knows."

"Here, here," said Danny.

They were supposed to be having a meeting with their tutor that afternoon to discuss the possibility of spending an extra year at university in light of what the wimpy professor called their 'unfortunate incident'. With that in mind, the thought of getting in thick with hardened criminals seemed like the lighter option.

Danny was enthusiastic about their adventure for two reasons. Firstly, like Mick and Dave, Danny hadn't lost interest in academia, but he had started to tire of it. Secondly, and more importantly, he saw this as a chance to strengthen his bond with his two friends after his display of

– and he hated to use the word – cowardice. He hated it, but he knew it was entirely appropriate.

He had got his drinking mostly in check, but Danny couldn't shake off the guilt and shame he felt for making a bolt for safety while a man was down. He had beaten himself up relentlessly over this, and he hadn't been able to talk to anyone about it because he was afraid people would judge him.

So for him, this was a chance to put things right at whatever cost.

"So this great blues singer made one fantastic record then disappeared, right?" said Mick, even though they'd been over this several times already.

"So it would seem," said Dave.

"Sounds fishy, if you ask me," said Mick.

"Me an' all, Mickey," said Dave wearily. "Me an' all."

"Just do one thing for me, will you Dave?" said Mick.

"Go on?"

"Try not to get us killed."

Chapter 22

It was a crisp and clear morning in sunny Grays, Thurrock. There was a lovely coastal breeze to clear the sinuses of those who were out and about on foot, giving them a feeling of ease and that all was right with the world. Business in the bustling town centre was good, especially in the jobcentre and the local McDonalds, where truants and shoplifters expressed warmth for their fellow man by holding doors open for any elderly people they passed as they went about their business of the day.

The frosts of the harsh winter gone by were now all but a distant memory, as were the credit card bills and the deep, dark depressions that usually followed the season of goodwill. A coastal café had its doors open, and a delighted passer-by heard the picked intro to The Beatles' *Here Comes the Sun* from a small tinny radio.

In short, it was the kind of day that made you feel

like you would live forever and probably enjoy much of it, too.

Or at least it would be, if you hadn't been up since 5:00 am mentoring a newbie who, to put it nicely, didn't know his arse from his elbow. This boy (and in the eyes of the Sarge he was definitely still that) made Inspector Clouseau seem like Hercule Poirot. Maskell had decided his newest recruit was bloody useless, and if he didn't pull his socks up soon, he would be writing a very serious letter to his mother. But being forced to hold hands with the police equivalent of Corporal Pike wasn't the only thing stopping this from being Ted Maskell's idea of a perfect day.

There was the troubling matter of the imminent death of his late best friend's only son Dave and his friends, Mick and Danny. The lads were good company, and Maskell had enjoyed jamming some blues tunes with them last night – but they weren't ready to deal with men like

Norman Layer.

Around midday, he decided it was time for his young colleague to attempt an independent patrol, maybe get his first nick. That's what he told him, anyway.

The real reason for sending the young lad off on his own like this was that Maskell needed a break from babysitting duties. He wanted to clear his head, maybe go and get an ice cream and some sea air. Maybe the young constable would wander off in a burst of stupidity, getting lost and perhaps never to return.

Shamefully, Maskell toyed briefly with the idea of sending him to Leggero's to do some looking around but then thought better of it. The new recruit was a coddled buffoon and The Sarge didn't like him much, but he hoped he would never come into contact with people like Norman Layer or Slouch – he wouldn't stand a chance.

Like many in the business of crime solving and detection, Ted Maskell had a nose for wrong-doing. He knew every street in the town (and in the county, in fact) and therefore he knew the whereabouts of Leggero's Bar and Restaurant, but he could always smell this nasty little establishment long before he saw it, and he could smell it now as he made his way along Coast Road. Today, he thought he might just choke.

When Maskell's mind wandered, he sometimes wished that the floods of 1953, the chaos and aftermath of which was one of Maskell's earliest memories, would come back to the area. The schools would have to close for a few days, he thought, and the pitch at his beloved Grays F.C would become waterlogged, and a home game might get cancelled. Worse, some if not all of the independent shops that still remained would be washed out of the town. But then so would the scum and the gunge that oozed out of places like Leggero's.

As usual, he kept his distance from the place and walked on the other side of the street, as he was alive today on the strict proviso that he took no interest in any of Layer's affairs. But any policeman who's ever been to the scene of a serious road accident knows that it's sometimes hard to look away from a grizzly scene.

He was disgusted by the cheap feel of the place and considered it an eyesore as he did all the low-end drinking dens that had sprung up across town and all over Essex since Norman Layer's rise to power. He hated the faux-Spanish lettering painted (actually clumsily splattered) across the display window in the front of the building and the cheap and nasty 'Spanish' guitar that hung there. He also hated the pack-animals that lurked outside there of a nighttime supposedly to make people feel safe.

He also hated the fact that it was open early and Dave, Danny and Mick were in there having a lunchtime drink.

220

NORMAN LAYER

Licensed to sell intoxicating liquor on or off these premises

So read the sign above the door to this unlovely establishment, much to two of the three amigos' delight (Mick remained nonplussed); for if all else failed they had gained some intelligence on their subject.

"Makes the SU bar seem nice," Danny said as he removed the slice of lime from his bottle of Corona beer with the faintest look of distaste.

They all drank the nasty stuff, but Dave had hoped for a pint of Estuary Lager as he always did in this part of the county. Sadly, fewer and fewer places seemed to sell it these days. This really was a ghastly little place. It was dark and dingy, with candles crudely shoved into wax-splattered wine bottles on each table in a poor attempt to give the place a tasteful, continental feel. There were also wicker chairs and faded *Toro Bravo* posters on each of the four walls. If this was supposed to conjure up thoughts, images and perhaps memories of Spain then it certainly did for Dave; it brought to mind the cheap, culture-free package holidays he'd had there as a boy, thankfully in the days before karaoke became popular (and he'd bet they did that in here, too).

At the far end of the bar, there was a sticky dance floor and some audio equipment that gave some boy-wonder the chance to earn money pressing STOP and START buttons for a few hours every night. For Dave, this said it all about the place.

They hadn't learnt much from the chap who served them the tequila-flavoured gut-rot they were now drinking, mainly because the greasy little oik had managed to take their orders, get their beers, take Dave's money and bring him his change without uttering a word. This was impressive when one considered that earlier on in their acquaintance he'd managed to inform Dave that they didn't

sell Estuary Ale and that there wasn't any lager on tap

either.

"I 'ate to say it boys but I think we've missed a trick

'ere," said Mick, and until the front door opened, it looked

like he might have been right.

Dave was lucky enough to be facing the entrance

from their table, and Mick had a side view. Danny was

sitting opposite Dave, facing him square-on, but he could

tell that whoever had come in was the chap whose face

Dave had recognised last night.

"Oh we haven't missed anything," said Dave.

Cutting an impressive and intimidating figure, the

big man in an even bigger leather jacket was without a

doubt the one in the photo on the back of the record sleeve.

"Reportin' for duty," he said to the rude man behind

the bar. "You can go and 'ave y' break now if you like," he

said.

This was his only communication with the barman, who shifted away without breaking his silence despite the esteemed company he was in. The big man took out a mobile phone and keyed in a number from memory.

"It's Slouch – where are you?" boomed the big man's voice.

There was a pause, and Dave, Danny and Mick silently mouthed the name they had just learnt.

"What do you mean yer in a meeting? 'Boss didn't say nothing to me. Then again he always did 'ave his favourites, didn't he. Okay, so I'm here on me tod until midnight?"

Dave nodded across the table to Danny, who grinned back at him.

"That's the last time I buy you breakfast," said Slouch before killing the call and sliding his phone back in the pocket he just took it from.

Danny gave Dave a wink then got to his feet or at least tried to, but he fell, purposely (though you'd never have known it), taking his chair and the table with him. It was a horrible sound, glass breaking and table legs screeching, but to Slouch it meant trouble. It was music to his ears.

Danny was as sober as a judge, but Dave and Mick had seen him drunk enough times to know that it was a splendid performance. He was humming *Land of Hope and Glory* as he began the supposedly difficult process of getting himself to his feet, but he was helped up by the gorilla-like man with the mobile phone and the bad attitude. Once Danny was upright, he swayed with such conviction it could have been his eighteenth birthday all over again.

"I say, unhand me you grubby proletarian!" he slurred in protest at his manhandling.

Slouch didn't know what the last word meant, but he knew he didn't like it. He hated big words, and he especially hated it when people smaller than him used them. He took Danny by his lapels and forced him against a nearby wall.

"One more word out of you," said the big man, not much louder than a whisper, his solid forehead only inches from Danny's nose and his eyes glassy with rage, "and you're a fucking dead man."

Pinned to the wall, Danny focused his mind and ignored the threat, even though he was close enough to smell the aftershave worn by the man who made it.

"Do you hear me? A FAKKIN' DEAD MAN!" Slouch's initial restraint left him, and he went from a whisper to a scream in an instant. He was breathing deeply, and Danny felt his massive frame expand and contract. Danny nodded to confirm he understood, and Slouch let him down and backed off a few feet.

"Now fuck off," said Slouch, not bothering to check the space behind him like the army had drummed into him many years earlier; he knew the other two wouldn't try anything stupid.

Dave and Mick got up and walked towards the exit. Danny went to do the same but was stopped in his tracks as Slouch put out an arm, mimicking a WWF clothesline manoeuvre.

"I'll cutcha' throat if you ever come in here again," Slouch said, his voice now a low murmur once more. "Now let me show you the door."

With that, he dragged Danny to the exit by his polo neck and threw him out like a rubbish sack. Mick and Dave were waiting for him when he landed in the street outside, and they were surprised to see him smiling as he got up and dusted himself off.

"That went rather well," he said, confusing them with his cheerful manner.

"Did it?" said Mick.

"Indeed it did, dear boy. Now walk with me – we could still be in danger."

They did as Danny said and walked until they came to a bus stop about a quarter-of-a-mile down the road from Leggero's. They sat down to discuss their progress so far.

"Well," said Danny, "I may have risked life and limb, and I may have stared into the cold face of death. But I found this."

He took an expensive black leather wallet out from his back pocket and held it up for the others to see. It wasn't his.

Mick looked on in amazement, but Dave was just mildly amused – he knew Danny had been up to something.

"Half-inching his wallet – I like it," said Dave. "I like it a lot."

"I didn't think he 'ad it in him," said Mick, shaking his head.

They all laughed.

Chapter 23

Back at the car that Dave had wisely parked several streets away from Leggero's, Danny handed the stolen wallet to Dave who fished out Slouch's driving licence. Now they had his address, too.

"Let's spin his drum!" Mick said to Dave, who must have been thinking the same thing since his car was already in gear and he was set to spin his wheels.

En route to this Slouch fella's house in the quaint Castle Point village of Thundersley, they stopped at a petrol station along the Benfleet-bound A127 to buy a disposable camera. As Danny went into the store, Mick told Dave he had read somewhere (*Loaded* magazine) that you could pick a Yale lock using only a large paper clip, a hammer, and a screwdriver.

"Look under y' seat" was all Dave had to say to that.

Mick looked under his seat but saw no paper clips, nor a hammer or a screwdriver (although there was an impressive toolkit in the boot, along with jumper cables, a two-litre bottle of water, a tartan blanket and a few other necessities). What he did see was a crowbar that lived under the passenger seat in case of attack, Dave being the fierce advocate of health and safety that he was.

"Wow," said Mick without picking it up. "You've done this sort of thing before."

Yes, unlike you two mummy's boys ...

"Might come in handy if he pops back for his sandwiches," said Mick.

***

They pulled over in a neighbouring village. It was tempting to drive around the block a few times and maybe even go past Slouch's house, but the street was a leafy, tree-lined affair and Dave knew that this could get them noticed.

"First thing we do is find out if anyone's home. I need a volunteer." This was Dave talking. "Mick," he said without looking at him.

"Yes, mate?"

"You're it – you can knock on the door for me. If anyone answers, pretend you're a pikey working in the area, and you've got the afternoon off. Just put on that Irish accent you sometimes do in the pub and ask if they've got a tree they'd like cutting down or if they've got any scrap that metal needs taking away – be creative. Hopefully, nobody will answer, and we can go about our business at a leisurely pace."

"One question," said Mick, knowing that refusal was pointless. "Why me?"

"Because you look more like a handyman than old soppy bollocks in the back 'ere." Dave paused for a moment while he had another brainwave (he was on *fire*

today). "Mind you, he'd make excellent Jehovah's witness.

Yeah, go on, joho, change of plan: we'll meet you there in

half-an-hour."

"You're sending me on foot?" asked Danny,

shocked and appalled.

"You could always steal a pushbike."

It felt harsh sending Danny on foot, but it was only

a mile or so. Dave knew neighbourhoods like this (though

he'd certainly never lived in one) and how they liked to

twitch their curtains now and again.

In a village where every other vehicle was an Audi,

Range Rover or Merc, Dave's Impreza would stand out like

a sore thumb, and he imagined that falling foul of the

Virginia Avenue Residents' Association (essentially a

modern-day village green preservation society) could be

more dangerous than the mission itself.

He mulled it over as he loop-the-looped around the well-manicured village green, knowing that even this was risking it.

"How the other 'arf live eh?" Mick pondered aloud, acknowledging that this was a world away from his and Dave's backyards.

"Yeah," said Dave, his eyes on the well-kept road. "Mind you, Danny probably thinks these are council houses."

Mick sniggered.

"Danny's a good kid," said Dave. "I know I'm tough on him sometimes, but he's one of us – he'll get there."

"I know," said Mick. "Mind you, we'd all leave our caravans and move in tomorrow if we could, right? That's why we do it, isn't it?"

Dave didn't have to think about this for long.

"Fuck tomorrow, mate – I'd move in tonight!" he

said.

This was something Dave had considered a good deal of late, especially since he'd started that silly degree course (which deep down he was rather enjoying). Was he a traitor? Was he selling out his own people?

Did he think he was better than them?

On the other hand, he owed it to his people to make the best of the few chances that came along, didn't he? Certainly, he knew that while manual work could be good for the soul, it wasn't always good for your back.

Either way, he had no time for all the champagne socialists he was forced to share air with on campus, with their Che Guevara posters and their trust funds. God, he hated them. Wankers, the lot of 'em.

Tired and overwhelmed, Dave was becoming lost in his thoughts, but he was brought back into the real world by the shrill ringing of his mobile. He held it to his ear without looking to see who was calling, being a responsible road user an' all.

"Dave, it's me, Danny." Dave noticed he sounded more excitable than usual.

"There's nobody in the house – well, nobody except me!"

"You what?"

"I'm in, Dave. I'm in the house – and you need to see this place."

Dave had made Danny leave his mobile in the car, and it took him about a second to work out that Danny must be calling from Slouch's home phone.

"See you in five," said Dave, impressed with his friend for gaining access to the house, yet stunned by his stupidity in giving a dangerous criminal his phone number.

He'd get a slap for that.

Those silly fuckers – why couldn't they just leave well alone?

This thought went through Ted Maskell's head when he'd seen his friends in the poky little 'tapas bar', and the same words came from his mouth as he'd got in his car to go and find his bumbling underling. The boy was relieved of his duty, and The Sarge complained to his skipper of a migraine and was sent home, missing work for only the second time in nearly thirty years.

Back at the house, the Sarge took a beer from his fridge and, foolishly, considering the circumstances, drained it one before fetching a repeat prescription.

He took his second cold Bud through to the living room of his modest bungalow, not far from the nick in Thurrock and cautioned himself (for a change) to slow down the drinking. He knew he would need his wits about him to get his friends out of this alive – if they weren't dead already.

One of Sergeant Maskell's strengths was that he was a doer rather than a thinker, and this set him apart from all of his younger colleagues. He would run a problem over in his mind several times, but only in preparation to act and not to avoid it as so many seemed to do these days. Once the right answer was found, however unpleasant or unpopular it was, this was what he acted upon.

Unless of course, it meant taking Norman Layer to task, in which case, as he ruefully admitted to himself from time to time, he would essentially turn a blind eye. On one occasion, he'd deliberately botched a high-profile investigation to save his own neck.

He rarely allowed himself to feel pity or shame over this, for that would have made him a pathetic individual; he still had *some* self-respect left. This was impressive, considering he knew deep down that by allowing Norman Layer to make him renege on his duty to the police, the Queen, his country and whatever else then he might as well have been working for him.

No, enough of all that. Maskell knew he might die

in his efforts to save his friends – they might die as a result of his actions – but inaction would mean certain death for all of them. At least he would die on his feet, which he now realised was better than living on your knees, as he'd been doing nearly all of his adult life thanks to Norman Stanley Layer.

He decided it was time to pull himself together. He'd go and see Dave and his mates tonight, tell them everything, get them to a place of safety, then …?

He could only wait and see.

He felt strangely elated at doing the right thing and standing up to the bastard at last. Plus, it dawned on him that Layer didn't have quite the full deck he once had; Maskell's wife was now dead anyway (or at least she was dead to him: she'd run off with the milkman years ago), and his two boys had grown into fine young men who could look after themselves.

"Yep," he said aloud, "the angels with the dirty

faces, no longer hold onto all the aces."

He reckoned his friends might like that line, and he decided there and then they could have it if they survived this long, dark night.

As he poured his beer down the sink, it also occurred to him that if Layer tried to kill him, which he would, for sure, then he would have no choice but to fight fire with fire and perhaps kill *him* first.

He was almost enjoying it now.

Chapter 24

Danny came to the door of 12 Virginia Ave holding a dry martini, greeting his friends and welcoming them over the threshold. He'd been pleasantly surprised to find the front door unlocked on arrival, and while he hadn't done much rummaging yet, he had found the drinks cabinet and rewarded his bravery with a small tipple.

"Entrer dans, entrer dans," he said as he gestured his friends in, grinning as he did so.

If Mick had been surprised at the *cojones* of his friend whose family had a Butler, then Dave was less so. He meant what he had said to Mick on their way over about Danny being one of them: he saw great potential in both of them, and he had done almost as long as he'd known them.

Dave had also seen alcoholism and despair of every kind in his twenty-seven years and could see exactly what Danny was battling with: his pride and his conscience.

Dave knew that the only cure for this was a dangerous challenge – preferably one that ended in a damn good scrap. As luck would have it, this seemed more likely by the minute.

Since Dave Hunter had made the life-changing decision to down tools and accept a scholarship, he'd been unimpressed with much of what he'd seen of university life so far. He'd expected the people there to lack the kind of grit and determination that he'd needed to survive in his old life and to not be particularly streetwise, and he'd been right in both cases. But he could live with that, and he was grateful for the chance to take a softer ride and perhaps flourish in a brains-over-brawn environment. So it wasn't this that had failed to impress; it was their sheer lack of substance that didn't do it for him. Many were not even especially committed to their studies and didn't afford any great respect to their lecturers who, while not exactly 'alphas' (not where he came from anyway), had been hired for a reason.

Thankfully, he'd befriended Mick and Danny early on in his academic career. Now, as then, he was grateful for their company (he was confident the three of them were going places too).

He'd also met a charming, elegant and very pretty young lady who played the saxophone with just the right combination of soul and skill and whom he liked very much. As did the 'Brooklyn bullshitter', who may well by now have 'done the deed' with this girl who he clearly had no respect for.

Dave knew Cooley Ritter had no respect for her and had known this since the first time Ritter and he had seen her, at their university induction day about a year-and-a-half ago.

She'd been the last one to join them in the SU bar that day, and no sooner had she sat down then Mr Ritter had somehow got her to himself and begun his pitiful life story. It was all *'I was a street corner kid, always hustlin', bustlin' and getttin' busted,'* then leading up to his miraculous recovery after finding redemption through *'this gift of music'*.

Nothing wrong with that, Dave thought, or at least there wouldn't have been anything wrong with it had Dave not heard what Mr Ritter had said *before* she sat at the table with them that day: *"Hey, look at Miss Prissy here; I bet she thinks she can piss perfume,"* and *"whoa, boy, a saxophone! That's not the only thing she'll be blowing this semester!"*

He'll get what's coming to him, Dave thought as he crossed the line from which he could never return and entered Slouch's home.

A few feet from the door was a large tiger skin rug, and Danny wondered if Slouch had killed the animal with his own hands. Beyond the tiger which might or might not have died of natural causes was the kitchen, a modern design largely at odds with the old-school thuggery of its owner. There were black oak panelled drawers with silver handles, a stainless steel commercial kitchen style hanger for utensils, grain effect vinyl flooring and a table island in the middle. There was also the homely smell of a recent fry-up, and this seemed more in keeping with the man they would all just have to get used to calling Slouch.

The living room, which was next door to the kitchen and faced the back garden, was plushly carpeted, well looked-after and gave hints of wealth and eccentricity also not in keeping with the thoroughly unpleasant chap they met earlier. There was an illuminated tropical fish tank in the living room, as well as a tank for an iguana and another that housed a giant python.

There was also, and this was truly a thing to behold, a wall-sized seven-by-seven-foot turtle cage, with at least three of the vicious, snappy little buggers visible against the camouflaging backdrop of what looked like Slouch's own private rainforest.

Danny wondered what names Slouch gave to these reptiles that neither he or his friends knew were rare hypo-pastel yellow-bellied sliders. They also didn't know that somewhere at the bottom of the slimy tank lurked an even rarer two-headed yellow-bellied slider, and anybody who had taken LSD at any time in their life did not want to see one of these.

Slouch also had installed a rather groovy-looking bar in the back corner, with a mirror ball hanging from the ceiling but thankfully without the word 'BAR' in neon-letters as favoured by many DIY alcohol enthusiasts. Next to the bar was a disco deck with a pair of speakers big enough for Wembley Arena, which must have gone down a bundle with the neighbours when they tuned in for the Last Night of the Proms.

"Looks like our man's a bit of a party animal," said Mick, surveying the scene.

"I'll say," said Dave as he licked his finger and dabbed it several times along the bar, before touching it to the tip of his tongue to confirm what he'd suspected: Slouch didn't treat his guests to sherbet dips.

"Result?" asked Mick.

"Yeah, silly fucker," said Dave, making no attempt to hide his contempt for drug users.

"Come on, let's check upstairs."

He led the way, and halfway up the stairs, on the wall, was a glass case that held a pair of giant katana swords. Mick shivered as he imagined what one of these could do if used in anger, and he photographed it as evidence.

Upstairs, they went into the master bedroom, which sat at the rear of the property overlooking the garden, home to Slouch's pond and his expensive collection of Japanese fish.

There was a row of coloured light bulbs on the

ceiling as well as a mirror positioned just above the bedpost. The wallpaper was patterned in black and purple, and there was a set of silver effect chrome dimmer switches by the bedside table.

The room reminded Dave of a scene from an old Goldie Hawn and Dudley Moore film, and he grinned as he wondered which of his assistants would open the cupboard and what might happen when they did.

Unsurprisingly, the bed was a waterbed, with leopard-skin linen and two black leather heart-shaped pillows. There were scratches along the metal frame of the bed that were quite possibly from the handcuffs now laying at the foot of the bed next to a Korean lashing cane that could make a man's eyes water just looking at it.

On the opposite wall stood another glass frame. This one contained a collection of throwing knives which, like the samurai swords and the cocaine, Dave thought would be of great interest to Ted Maskell and his friends down at the station.

Instinctively and without looking, Mick reached under the bed. He pulled out a shiny black leather briefcase and put it on the bed for his friends to see. It had a gold combination lock, and four correct digits would be required to open it.

Danny took out Slouch's driving licence and read out the date of birth to Mick, who knelt down and got to work. They tried date and month without joy. Then month and year – still no joy. They tried date and year, year and date and every other variation on the big man's birthday. Still, the wretched thing wouldn't open.

"Maybe he's not as daft as he looks," said Mick matter-of-factly, not one to show emotion.

"Yeah, but he's none too clever either," said Dave.

"Enlighten us," said Mick.

"Did neither of you see the calendar on the kitchen wall?"

"What, the one with all those *Asian birds* with their *tits* out?" asked Danny, his face squeezed with excitement like a young Rik Mayall.

"Yes, Danny, the one with all those Asian birds with their tits out – that's assuming they are birds and not 'Bangkok chick boys'. Anyway, the last day of this month was marked as *Mum's birthday*."

"How many days in April?" asked Mick.

"Thirty days, Michael – Thirty days!"

Dave took a deep calming breath and reminded himself to stay focused despite this having been an above-averagely exciting day.

Mick opened the case on his first attempt with the new numbers, and inside was a wad of used notes, a scalpel, a small revolver and enough cocaine for a Led Zeppelin aftershow.

Mick held up one of the bags of white powder. "Maybe he's planning a surprise party for his mum," he said before he looked under the bed and found nine more briefcases, each identical to the one he'd just opened.

"Right then, boys," said Dave. "Let's get the fuck out of here."

"Eh?" said Danny, confused.

"Aren't we gonna take this as evidence?" said Mick.

"Or these weapons?" said Danny, gesturing to the knives on the bedroom wall but referring more to the deadly swords on the stairway or perhaps Slouch's S&M lashing cane.

"No," said Dave, turning his back on the men. "If we give this to the old bill, it'll mean nothing. They might even think we put this stuff here ourselves."

"So we make an anonymous call?" said Danny.

Dave shook his head again.

"He'll end up inside, where he'll be as much use to us as a shovel in a shitstorm. And," he said, turning to face

251

the other two, "we still know four-fifths of fuck all about Fulton's murder."

"Murder? Who said anything about murder, Dave?"

It was Mick who asked the question, but Danny was thinking the same thing.

"I don't think these are the kind of people that use sarcasm, do you?"

Mick shook his head in reluctant agreement.

"Me neither," said Dave. "Here's what we do. We photograph the drugs, we photograph the swords, we photograph his knives, we get the fuck out of here, and we see what happens next. If we're lucky, he'll come to us. Now, gentlemen, I say we foxtrot oscar."

Mick did as Dave said and snapped the incriminating items in the bedroom. Satisfied with the evidence, Dave led the way.

He started out purposefully but stopped on the landing with a look on his face that was a little bit like fear, as he realised they didn't have the place to themselves after all.

Chapter 25

"I think we might have a problem here, boys," said Dave, playing the situation down a bit.

He was looking at the biggest, ugliest and the most hateful-looking dog he'd ever seen. It was the kind of dog that made the papers now and again, could kill you easily and for fun and had probably been named Brutus or Rambo by its irresponsible owner, even though Dave thought Cerberus might be more appropriate.

The hellish beast's fur was jet black save for a few bursts of auburn around his pointy Mau-cat ears. He (it was definitely a he, and although he was crouched you just knew he had a dick like a horse), had a muzzle shaped mouth that thankfully was shut right now. He was longer than he was tall despite being over two-and-a-half feet at the shoulder. Old Cerberus was well-built, too; he was toned like a horse as well being hung like one.

Dave remembered reading somewhere that the Roman army had used dogs like these as they were truly fearless beings. He'd read that swords or spears could do nothing to deter one of these bastards once its blood was up, and for the first time in his life, he wished Barney from The Red Lion was around.

Actually, it was the first time he'd ever thought of Barney away from the pub.

The dog had a constant low growl like the rumble of a high-performance motorbike ticking over before a race. If this made Dave feel uneasy it was nothing compared to the sight of it baring its teeth. Dave kept his eyes open but avoided direct eye contact with the beast as per Barney's instructions.

Mick, hearing the growl and seeing Dave's frozen stance understood what was happening, even if he couldn't see the hellhound that might soon be on his trail. He reached for the cabinet containing the throwing knives, but

Danny held up his arm to signal him to stop: he had a better idea.

Danny picked the Korean lashing cane up from the bed and handed it to Mick, who passed it nice and slowly to Dave, who was grateful for an alternative to the next part of Barney's dog defence manual.

Dave took the kinky weapon and raised it above his head, then brought it down between him and the attack dog. The whip made a loud, swooping 'whoosh' sound as it sliced the air in front of him and scared the dog a bit. Good, Dave thought. It's working.

The deadly canine inched back but maintained its menacing stance. Now, Dave made eye contact with the animal as he brought the cane down with even greater force than before, and Cerberus jumped back a foot or so.

The door to Slouch's bathroom was another three feet back from where the dog was standing. The door had been left open, and if Dave could just maintain the upper hand for a moment longer, they could shut him in and be on their way.

"Eye of the tiger, son, eye of the tiger," he said as he brought his whip up once more, then down again with all the force he could muster.

With the mighty crack that followed, the dog abandoned its 'crouching tiger' position and retreated into the bathroom and into the bathtub where it tried to hide; Dave felt like a bit of a bully, but he knew he'd only done what was necessary.

He slammed the door shut and imprisoned the great beast, then the three of them beat a hasty retreat from the house, stopping only to photograph Slouch's deadly samurai swords as they went.

They headed for the coast, Southend-on-Sea being the spiritual home of one David Ian Hunter as well as a close and convenient place for them to rest up. There was relief at being back from behind enemy lines, but there was also a cockiness about them which could only come from having faced danger – something that at least one of them had never done before today.

Dave could see a change in his younger friends. Their attitude and their stance was different, and there was a hint of swagger about them. It was a change for the better and he liked it.

Of course, it wasn't hard to see why people who put their necks on the line felt they walked taller than those who preferred to play it safe, Dave thought as he drove. In the case of early man, it was only right that the men who ventured outside their caves to find food for their families (and at the same time risked becoming dinner for the sabre-toothed tigers) had first pick of the cavewomen upon their return.

Enjoying this train of thought, Dave jumped forward forty million years or so to his own lifetime or more specifically his childhood. Impressed by his late father's friend's tales of law-enforcement, he'd thought about joining up once he made the transition to manhood (something Dave spent his entire boyhood champing at the bit for, unlike those little wankers on campus, he reflected).

When he'd asked Ted Maskell what sort of qualities they looked for in new recruits, his response had been simple yet had summed it up perfectly: "Well, son," he'd said, puffing his cigar, this being Christmas and the era before political correctness came along and ruined everything, "you run to things that most people run from."

It was the best lesson Dave Hunter ever learnt, even if he hadn't known it at the time, being six years old and everything. But he realised it soon after, and the events of today reminded him of this timely advice from the legendary hard-man, Ted Maskell.

In fact, Dave was starting to see now why he was sometimes resentful towards the people he encountered at university. They all wanted to go far, wanted to be the cream of the crop, for sure they did. But they didn't want to put themselves on the line, to tough it out and take risks: they wanted gain without pain.

And the worst thing was? They'd probably get it.

As Dave's car bobbed along Southend's sticky mile, he listened to Danny and Mick squabbling in the back like the two old women they really were. Wanting to drown them out, he switched the radio on and was delighted to hear Johnnie Walker introducing Dr Feelgood's *She Does It Right*, the three-minutes-and-twenty-seconds of which would surely see out the remainder of the journey. And if they were still at it then?

He could throw them off a waltzer, couldn't he.

Dave parked up along the Western Esplanade, and they walked the half-mile or so to the famous Southend Pier, with Dave catching awestruck glimpses of the nearby Cliffs Pavilion as they went. To some, this was just a provincial matinee theatre, the likes of which you often saw in British seaside towns; to Dave Hunter, it was a kind of Mecca.

He'd seen many world-class musicians here: BB King; Jools Holland; John Mayall; local lads Dr Feelgood, and The Pirates; The Everly Brothers; Little Richard … The list was long. Great shows, great artists and great memories.

Cliffs Pavilion was the perfect size for a live music venue, whereas places like Birmingham NEC made the artists look like Subbuteo figures to most of the audience. Great, so you either looked at a guitar-playing midget or a cinema screen, the latter being something Dave had flatly refused to do on the handful of occasions he'd been to one of these dumps.

No, Cliffs Pavilion was where it was at, and Dave was sure of it. Here, you saw the musicians in all their glory, saw them breathe and sweat before your very eyes.

This was where musicians became larger than life which was surely the point after all. He was also sure – make that damn sure – that he would play there one day.

Norman Layer was approaching the eighteenth hole of his course and was just a few putts away from declaring victory over his 'friend', 'Left-Handed' Pete, who had not enjoyed his exclusive session with the chief, as nobody did bar maybe their first.

The problem with playing golf with the boss was that while it was bad form to win, you couldn't be seen to let him win either. If Norman Layer had an Achilles heel then this was it: he had never heard the tale of the emperor's new clothes. Or, to use modern parlance, he didn't see the danger in playing out your life as one big dick-measuring contest. For having proved that yours was biggest of all, there was a tendency to expect others to drop to their knees and suck it for you. Big mistake – your employees will start telling you what you want to hear rather than what you need to: yes-men rarely say no.

This wasn't really a problem when you played a few holes with your boss, who was semi-retired and owned a golf course, but that didn't mean 'Left-Handed' Pete hadn't wished the wind would pick up and carry some of his shots wide that morning.

With his eye on his drive but his mind on the problem, Norman Layer asked 'Left-Handed' Pete the million-dollar question. "Are you sure Slouch isn't going to fall apart on me?"

"He'll be fine, chief. I know he's not been 'imself lately, but then he's always been a miserable sod, hasn't he? I'll keep an eye on him for you."

As soon as the words left his mouth, he knew this had been the wrong thing to say, and as Layer swung his club, 'Left-Handed' Pete had a shuddering vision of someone's nose being used as a tee for the Slazenger ball. Layer's 9-iron made its connection, and the ball headed into the distance while tufts of grass flew upwards then fluttered down gracefully.

The two of them walked fifty yards to the next shot, with their loyal caddy behind them trying not to overhear their conversation. Pedro's English wasn't good, and he'd been hired for that reason, but he had enough sense to work out that his boss didn't sell ice creams for a living.

Pete reminded himself that the boss often got like this before a job, even though he had noticed that Slouch had seemed distant of late, which was dangerous considering the circumstances (and, in Norman Layer's eyes, more than a bit ungrateful since this was the chance of a lifetime).

"I've seen this before," said Mr Layer as he lined up his next putt. "People change as they get older; they go soft, start seeking redemption. You'd be surprised how many people find God once they start getting closer to 'im.'"

To an innocent bystander, it would seem bizarre that on a day like this, when the sun was out, and the sky was blue, and a soft breeze was blowing along the fairway, anyone could think about pulling a gun on another human being. If a nice, normal person was reading the newspaper over elevenses and a story involving an act of inhumanity turned up, they would just turn over to the Sudoku page or the gossip column. For even without a pretty girl by your side and a glass of something chilled and refreshing in your hand, it was the kind of day that should fill you with love for life.

Of course, it was their talent for violence that allowed men like Norman Layer and 'Left-Handed' Pete to live the lifestyle they did; not many people who earned an honest living could reach for the clubs and break off for a round of golf any time they felt like it. And if they could, then it was unlikely they'd own the lodge, the fairway and all of its eighteen holes.

"A fella named John McCraig used to work for me – big Johnny Mac they used to call him. He used to box around fairgrounds in the sixties – big Irishman 'e was," said Layer, now looking his golf buddy right in the eye.

"What happened?" asked Pete, half-knowing the answer.

"He went off and joined a monastery."

Pete didn't know if he was meant to laugh and still didn't after what came next.

"Mind you he was a pikey, so he might've been after the lead in the roof."

"Yeah, well, old habits an' all that," said Pete, not sure why he needed to know all this.

Layer was lining up his next shot when his mobile phone rang.

"Speak o' the devil," he said when he realised who

it was (it was Slouch, and Pete didn't think for a second it was this Johnny Mac that Norman Layer had just been talking about).

Layer listened for about a minute, and Pete watched the colour drain from his face.

After half a mile or so, Dave, Mick and Danny reached the entrance to the pier. Dave liked Southend Pier, and he liked it a lot.

It was hard not to like a place like this on a sunny day. Even before summer was in, the place was awash with smiling faces, and filled with the echoing sounds of merry-go-rounds and laughter. Everywhere you looked there were memories: old memories being relived and colourful new ones being made.

It was hard not to get caught up in it all, so alive it was and so alive it made you feel.

Dave told Mick and Danny that they weren't

allowed a go on the dodgems or the shooting range, as they were only having a moment's downtime or a working lunch if they could find a queue for fish and chips that wasn't longer than the pier itself.

On a serious note, Dave could see they were in danger of becoming demob-happy just as their mission was just getting underway. He would soon do something about that.

Chapter 26

It was peaceful and serene at the end of the world's longest pier, where the crashing of the waves below and the seagulls above provided a mellow alternative to the sensory overload of the modern world. Here, there were no car horns, no mobile phones, no talentless television pop star wannabes and no students quoting Monty Python wrongly.

An elderly lady was knitting on a little wooden bench while nearby her husband cast a line from his fishing rod. As there was at the end of any pier in Great Britain, whatever the weather and whatever the time of the year.

In short, it was a lovely escape from it all for anybody with the wisdom to seek out such a thing. Or at least it was until the three stooges rocked up, armed with fish and chips and a rowdy exuberance. And four cans of Carling bought from the same petrol station as the disposable camera, after Danny misinterpreted Dave's suggestion that they stock up on tinned goods in case they had to go into hiding.

They sat down on a wooden bench, on the side of the pier opposite the elderly couple (even though it was unlikely they had ties to Slouch or Norman Layer) and began their working lunch.

"Right then," said Mick, sounding rather pleased with himself. "We know Slouch deals, owns illegal weapons, keeps a big dog and he's a kinky old bastard," he said while using his fingers to count up the offences. "Not bad for a morning's work."

Danny joined in. "And *we've* got the evidence," he said proudly.

"All here on candid camera," said Mick, tapping the pocket of his denim jacket where he kept the camera that held the supposedly incriminating images.

"Here, let's have a look at that," said Dave, gesturing that he wanted the camera. He took it and looked at it for a second. "Disposable camera, eh?" he said, before standing it up and hurling it into the Estuary.

Danny was the first to react.

"Did he just …?" he said, eyes wide, mouth agape.

Mick threw his battered sausage and chips to the floor and pulled himself up to face Dave square on.

"What the *fuck* did you do that for!?"

The elderly lady nearby seemed not to notice, and neither did her husband, who was about to bring in the biggest catch of his career even if it was an old Dr Marten boot, a relic from the golden era in the region's history where mods and rockers would gather here to beat the shit out of each other.

"Cool it, Michael, cool it," said Dave, steady as a mountain, his hands held up in a calming gesture. "Let's not forget we're here to find out about a missing blues singer and to find out what our friend Ted Maskell's involvement was – or is."

"*Your* friend Ted Maskell," Mick said.

Dave ignored that.

"Look, at least we know the kind of people we're dealing with now, right?"

A not-even-half-hearted 'if you say so' was the best that Mick could manage.

"Those pictures would have got us arrested. And in the nick, we'd be sitting ducks for someone like him, believe me."

Dave didn't know if this was true or not. The one time he'd been arrested, he'd been in a solitary cell where he'd felt as safe as proverbial houses, but this line sounded good so he used it anyway. Plus he'd seen the film *Goodfellas,* and he knew Mick Davies had too.

He could see it was working.

"I think Bobby Fulton was killed. We all thought it, didn't we? hc said.

Mick and Danny both nodded.

"And it doesn't take Inspector Morse to work out that The Sarge is mixed up in all of this." He paused for a while, impressed with his leadership skills and equally impressed with his recruits for having the ability to see sense so quickly after a minor diversion.

Dave put his ability to reason with others down to the fact that he was good at reasoning with himself; if nothing else, he was decisive and not one to avoid a difficult conclusion if need be. That's why he threw the camera into the sea when a lesser man would have clung to that one lead for the little – and false – comfort it gave.

"I've known The Sarge all me' life, and he's a good man … He taught me everything I know about blues harmonica. It ain't right for a big fella like him to be scared like this." His voice cracked as he said this, which was convenient as it saved him having to fake it (some people were suckers for a pair of sad eyes, he thought).

"So," he said. "Are we back in business?"

273

"Yeah, go on then," said Mick. "You'll only mess it up on your own."

"That's the spirit. Danny?"

Danny was enjoying this far too much to back out now, yet he said nothing.

Instead, he held out his right hand for the others to follow suit, and they stacked their hands to renew the blood oath they had all taken when they got in the car that morning. The boys were back in town.

Such ceremony was hardly necessary, but boys will be boys, and Essex ones even more so.

"The three amigos ride again!" said Dave, playing it cool as ever.

"So what now?" asked Mick, keen to get things started again.

"Sarge comes off shift at about five. I say we lay low for a couple of hours, then we go to his gaff. We tell him what we've found, we tell him what we know, and we make him tell us what he knows. We could also swing by the local library and see if we can find any old press cuttings to do with Fulton's disappearance."

Almost the second that Dave mentioned The Sarge, his mobile rang. It was the man himself, sounding like he was in a phone box and as serious as a heart attack.

"'Allo, Sarge."

"Shut up and start listening."

"Blimey, Sarge, did you get out the wrong side o' bed this morning?"

"That's not shutting up, and it's not fucking listening. Shut up and listen, you stupid boy."

Dave went quiet for the first time in a long while and started listening.

"I don't know what you and your friends are playing at, but it stops, and it stops now."

There was a silence while Maskell composed himself and got his breath back. "Keep away from

Leggero's, and any other licensed premises in the county. Understand?"

"Yeah, sure. What's all th –?"

The Sarge talked straight over him.

"Forget about Bobby Fulton, keep away from the man who calls himself Slouch and keep the fuck away from Norman Layer. Where are you now?"

"Southend Pier, Sarge."

"For fuck's sake … Norman Layer *owns* Southend Pier."

Beginning to appreciate the seriousness of the situation, Dave started scanning the area for shifty-looking men carrying bunches of flowers.

"Go home, lock your doors and just play dead. I'll be there once I've worked out how I'm gonna do this," said The Sarge.

"Do what?" Dave asked.

"How I'm gonna get you out of this alive."

And with that, the line went dead.

Chapter 27

They parked two streets away from Dave's house. Mick had driven since Dave, ostensibly the worldliest of the trio had wanted to keep an eye out to see if they'd been followed. Dave looked at his watch and allowed one minute to pass before beginning the task of getting them back to the house.

"Follow me, boys – I've got a plan."

Dave lived in a street corner house. His front door, which he didn't fancy using at that moment for fear of being shot dead, was on the main drag off Colchester's London Road. The other side of the property faced a quiet side street, which they could get to from where they had parked via an overgrown yet passable footpath. They hurried along the path and emerged opposite a house two doors along from Dave's.

The neighbour-but-one had a walkway between his

and the house next door, and Dave motioned for them to follow him along this route.

It was 7:00 pm – dusk. This meant that Dave, Mick and Danny could see what they were doing, but Dave was aware that this meant others could see them.

At the end of the passageway, they came to a coal bunker. A quick climb and a jump and the three of them were in the neighbour's yard in a jiffy, and there were no skateboards or unchained dogs there waiting to spoil their plans.

The garden was enclosed with sliding wooden fence panels, and Dave raced to the last one, on the opposite side to the coal bunker. It was a new panel which hadn't yet taken to its soil base. Lifting it was easy enough, and he held it halfway up while Mick slide-tackled his way under. Danny dived through like a convict making a bolt for freedom before Dave let the weight go and rolled under.

***

279

They waited upstairs in the spare room that housed Dave's record collection, puffing on cigarettes but by no means drinking beer or any other kind of alcoholic booze: Ted Maskell hadn't had to tell them that. They sat in darkness, and the sound of a nearby owl took away the need for Danny to impersonate one.

Dave didn't like being in hiding; he felt like they were running away, but he had to respect the Sergeant's wishes – for now, anyway. They could have waited downstairs, but that would have meant either drawing the curtains – which suggests someone is home – or sitting there with them open for all to see; Dave had incurred the wrath of Sergeant Maskell once today.

Once darkness fell, around twenty-hundred hours, they ventured downstairs, and Dave drew the curtains as one might do at that time, using only his portable TV to light the room to a modest degree, having turned it to face the wall before he switched it on.

Five minutes later, they heard a knock at the door. Mick peered through the curtains. It was The Sarge.

Dave let him in, and nobody failed to notice Maskell's lack of customary cheer. He was out of uniform, wearing a thin black leather jacket, black jeans and black running shoes, showing complete disregard for all the school road safety talks he'd given over the years.

In the living room, Mick and Danny sat, but Dave and The Sarge preferred to stand.

"All I can say is you've been bloody stupid. You boys are young – don't get me wrong, I was looking forward to seeing my pension next year, but you had your whole lives ahead of you."

Even Danny noticed his use of past tense.

Dave looked at his friend jaw-to-jaw.

"I think it's time you told us everything."

Maskell, more used to saying this than hearing it, sighed as if to say 'Ok, what the hell,' with a hint of 'we'll be dead soon anyway so what does it matter'. "OK," he said. "I've got my will in order." He looked right back at Dave. "Just don't think you're gonna live to tell the tale."

A Mercedes van took the Colchester exit and thundered down the slip road, carrying three men with hearts as black as the vehicle's paintwork. Barry Wise gripped his 'army surplus' (an underworld nickname for a weapon stolen and reported lost by rogue servicemen then sold on the black market, in his case a lethal Heckler and Koch machine gun that could carve you up like a turkey at Christmas). His colleagues Shark and Frankie Howse had to make do with sawn-offs that had been obtained in the same illegal manner. The driver was Ron Butler, and if the shooters gave him nerves, then he didn't show it.

They drove in close formation with a Blue BMW driven by Phil Howlens, in which Slouch took the passenger seat, and 'Left-Handed' Pete rode in the back.

For most of the journey, nobody had said much; now Slouch and 'Left-Handed' Pete were killing time by fixing sound-suppressing tubes to their shotgun barrels.

Dave offered Maskell a cigarette. The Sarge had been battling nicotine addiction for many years, but saving five minutes of his life now seemed like small beer. He took it, and Dave sparked his lighter for him.

"Bobby Fulton was a friend of mine – a good friend, in fact," he said, before taking a long drag on his cigarette. "He was a friend of your dad's, too."

"My Dad?" asked Dave, "did this –"

"Have anything to do with him?" Maskell asked, finishing the question for him. "No. I can assure you, David, your father had nothing to do with any of this – he was too clever for that."

Satisfied that his friend took his word for it, the story began.

"Everyone loved Bobby back in the 70s, and everyone knew he was going places. I used to roadie for him – we used to hang out, chase crumpet together. We used to jam a lot, too. They were good days."

He took another drag on his cigarette and coughed.

"Still, time went by, and we went in other directions. That's life for you, I'm afraid. I joined up, got married, started a family. I kept my hand in, but I knew what side my bread was buttered on, and I knew my future lay in nicking people. As for Bobby, well, he wanted the lot. Fast cars, fast women, load o' money, big old house in the country – he nearly got it, too. What he couldn't do was get signed up – he couldn't get a recording contract for love nor money," he said, exasperated at the music business, something Dave could relate to in spite of the very different lives that he and The Sarge led.

"Labels wouldn't touch him, said he was too old-fashioned. Also, he liked a drink, and 'e could get a bit lively once in a while. Not aggressive as such, but he didn't suffer fools if you know what I mean. All this time I was getting my feet under the table with the old bill – I was makin' a bit of a name for meself, too. Anyway, the name on everyone's lips back then was Norman Layer. Cor, 'e was a nasty piece of work." The Sarge frowned and shook his head at the mere mention of this name. "Every bloke on the force back then wanted to be the one to bring 'im down. They would've done an' all, but he was too good, too clever – not to mention too dangerous."

It was unlike Danny to sit still for any length of time, but he was gripped by Maskell's narrative and was hanging on his every word. Mick shifted in his seat, like someone watching a movie during a scene where it looks like the hero might die; Dave played it cool, of course, but even he was wondering if he had done the right thing in starting this very personal, very private investigation.

"Anyway, Bobby's back in the country in '76, year

285

of the heatwave. He's been on the continent with Status Quo all summer, passing it about, having a right old time, but now he's back in England, and he can't get arrested. So, him and his band get themselves a booking at The Broadway Club down on the sticky mile, where they go down a storm with the punters and catch the ear of the club's owner."

"Layer?" asked Mick?

"I'm afraid so, my friend. I'm afraid so. He offers the world to poor old Bobby who, let's remember, is down on his luck.

He offers him a residency at The Broadway Club, has him sing at his parties, gets him bookings in all his clubs, buys him champagne, gets him a flash motor … Well, it's everything he wanted."

Hearing this made Dave think of the late, great Robert Johnson, standing at the crossroads, waiting for a man in a dark cloak to appear and make him an offer he can't refuse. It saddened Dave that after all these years people still hadn't learned to beware of strangers bearing gifts.

It was their own fault, of course, but that didn't stop Dave feeling sorry for this great singer he'd never known and never would, for he had already worked out how the story would end.

"So the next thing you know, Norman Layer's got Bobby under his wing, and all seems to be going well. Bobby even called me, asked if I wanted to come to see him at The Broadway Club, New Year's Eve, 1977."

"Was that the last time you saw him?" asked Dave.

"I didn't go. I knew who owned The Broadway Club, and I wouldn't frequent an establishment run by criminals. Not then, not now." He said this with the conviction of a priest.

"Early '78, Layer realises he's onto a good thing with my old mate Bobby, and he wonders where he can take him next. Knowing that Bobby can't get a record deal, he sets up his own label. Who'd've thought it, eh?"

"A record label?" asked Danny, incredulous.

"That's right – he was quite the entrepreneur, Norman Layer. He was never afraid to think big, credit where it's due," he said, his tone sarcastic for the last bit. "I don't think he intended to wrong him as such, he just wanted to make some money and leave his mark. And if it failed, well, he'd have a tidy front for his drug money – perfect." He flicked the long ash off the cigarette he'd lost interest in.

"So what happened?" asked Dave, having guessed the answer in advance.

"Well, they put a record out. It was the one you showed me, in fact – I never did hear it. Anyway, it didn't take off here, and from what I gather it didn't do much in the States either. But it was believed to have sold over a million in Japan and Australia."

"Out of interest, how do you know all this?" asked Mick.

"It's what Bobby told me in late '79. People didn't use Citizens Advice back then, and 'cos I'm his mate – and I'm a copper – well, he called me up asking for help, didn't he. He reckoned money was going missing and all sorts. He told me he was being kept in the dark about record sales, and he reckoned he wasn't even told about the million-plus sales down under."

"What did you tell him?" asked Mick, again.

"I told him I didn't want to know. I told him he'd done this to himself, and unless he had a crime to report, he could leave me well alone. Only, he wouldn't let it go, and he starts rattling on about missing money and accounts and how he'd been doing some digging and how he was gonna get some answers … I put the phone down in the end. Like I said, I didn't wanna know. Of course, Norman Layer was building his golfing lodge at the time, which is where I reckon a lot of the money was going. The trouble is, Bobby sounded wired – paranoid, even – when he talked to me about all this, and it wasn't hard to work out why." He paused and looked Dave square in the face.

"Chances are he was on coke. It'd be like Norman Layer to give you all the drugs and all the lifestyle accessories you wanted, but what you *didn't* do was question him."

"Which Fulton did?" asked Danny.

"Like I said, he didn't suffer fools. My guess is, and let's not forget I've been around the block a few times, Bobby wanted to know where the money was going. He wanted answers. I reckon he looked into having the Matchbox accounts audited then told Norman Layer about it. That, or he threatened to blow the lid on Norman Layer's thriving drugs enterprise."

He paused to let his friends take all of this in, knowing only too well how tiring a long confession at the end of an even longer case can be. Dave held out the ashtray for Sarge who had abandoned his cigarette.

"Bobby was last seen in public on November 12th, 1979. Layer arranged a night out at Romford dogs, took a few of his staff and clients along. He liked doing things like that, chance to flash his money about, 'ave a flutter here and there. Surprise, surprise, he seldom lost a bet.

"Bobby was a bit of a local hero, so there was more pressure than usual to solve the case. I was a newly promoted inspector at the time, and I was assigned to lead the investigation into his disappearance – my first big job, you could say."

Maskell took a deep breath before beginning the most important part of the story, knowing that doing so would unearth memories he had tried to bury long ago.

"About two weeks into the investigation, I received a visit. Layer and a couple of his sidekicks – one of whom you met today, by the way – came to my house in the dead of night. They held Janice and me down while Norman Layer gave me some spiel about wanting to know too much. He told me how he went to Sunday school as a boy, and whenever he questioned the teachings of the priest he'd be beaten and locked in a cupboard to think about what he'd done. He said this was how he learned it could be dangerous to want to know too much. Then, he told me Bobby Fulton got into trouble for asking questions. Again, wantin' to know too much. That's when he told me what he'd done to him."

He took a long, deep breath. This was hard for him, but he was determined to get it all out.

"He told me people like Bobby Fulton didn't deserve to rest in peace, so they stuck him in the Hammersmith flyover where all the cars and lorries would keep him awake. Then, him and his thugs took out canisters of petrol and doused the bed with my wife and me still in it. My boys were asleep in the room next door, and he told me that once he was done with us, he was gonna go through and sing them to sleep." He paused briefly, but this did little to prepare them for what came next. "He started rattling a box of matches, singing *'Daddy's burning, daddy's burning ...'"*

Maskell's voice cracked as he recounted this, and he had to take a break for a moment. Nobody said anything, and Dave, Danny and Mick sat and quietly pondered what it must be like to live with a soul as darkly stained as this.

The Sarge took a few deep breaths and used his palms to dab his eyes. He had a story to finish, and Norman Layer wasn't going to get the last word this time.

"I was warned to back off the case, or I'd get another visit, only this time they'd strike a match and finish the job."

"And what did you do?" asked Danny, grimly fascinated.

"I botched the investigation," he said in a matter-of

fact way that failed to mask his shame. "The only person who came forward claiming to know anything was a fella named Martin – Martin Russell. He'd played in Bobby's band a few times. He called me at home, wanting me to go and meet him – he reckoned he knew something, but he wanted to tell me in person. Let's not forget, this was after Layer had been round and threatened to turn my bedroom into a crematorium."

"Let me guess," said Dave, "you scared him off?"

"Not exactly, no. I just told him that anything he told me would be useless unless he was prepared to speak out against Norman Layer in court, and since there was no proof or suggestion of any wrongdoing on Layer's part, we wouldn't be able to offer him protection either. I also told him that since he was a coloured fella, no-one would listen to him anyway." He hung his head in shame at what he had just said and what he had said all those years ago.

"What became of him?" asked Mick.

"He left the area – at least I hope that's what happened to him. Either way, I ain't heard a dickie bird from 'im since and I haven't been sittin' by the phone waiting for him to call either."

"Was Fulton married?" asked Dave, trying to keep up with all this. "I'm trying to work out who reported him missing."

"He was shacked up with a lady named Ruby, big-chested Caribbean girl, used to sing with Bobby over at the Broadway club – I think she was in on it, meself."

"Because she worked for Layer?" asked Dave.

"Yep, same as everyone did back then."

"Meaning?" said Dave.

"He had people everywhere. Certainly, he'd got at least one of his lackeys in every nick in the county. I know this because one of them came to see me in my office the day after they came to my house. Some cocky little fucker who was barely out of short trousers asked me if I slept well. Then he looked me in the eye, bold as brass, and read me the riot act. He told me I was to see to it that the Fulton investigation didn't go anywhere and that I must resign from my promotion to inspector. He also told me to keep away from all premises owned by Mr Layer, and that I was to keep out of any of his affairs and that I was never to rise above the rank of sergeant again."

"What about your friends on the square?" asked Dave hopefully. "Half the blokes from your lodge are coppers – they all think highly of you, don't they?"

Maskell shook his head and explained that while his friends within the Masonic community did hold him in high regard, Norman Layer was also a mason and one that was several steps higher up the table than him. Dave felt embarrassed for making a suggestion that not even Danny would have bothered with, so predictable was Maskell's answer.

"Sounds like he's got you right where he wants

you," said Danny, stating the obvious and showing little in the way of tact.

Maskell wasn't bothered – he knew it anyway.

"He's got eyes and ears everywhere. Whenever I went to a new nick, there was someone was waiting to introduce themselves, telling me the boss sends his regards."

He shook his head in disbelief as his mood shifted from despair towards something more befitting a man of his stature.

"Those little fuckers … They took an oath to Her Majesty the Queen. And who do they answer to? Norman fucking Layer, that's who."

Dave picked up this trace of anger in his friend's voice, and he knew this was the broken man's last hope; perhaps Ted Maskell had the fighting spirit that only a lucky few are born with.

"So what do we do?" Dave asked him.

"You're gonna get in the car with me, and we're gonna leave town while I see if I can get us out of this mess."

"Where to?"

"I've got a friend who transferred to Cambridge a few years back, fancied the quiet life. I can only assume Layer's men haven't got that far, and even if they have then Robbie Burnham's the kind of bloke who'd tell 'em to sling their hooks and piss off anyway."

"Just one thing," said Dave, "how do you plan to prove all this? How are you gonna prove he came and threatened to torch your house … Twenty-five years ago or whenever it was?"

"Got it all right here," said The Sarge, tapping the left-breast pocket of his jacket before taking an old police-issue dictaphone out from it.

"When I heard 'em coming up the stairs I hit record and left it in my bedside drawer – instinct, I guess. I assume it still works – I don't play it very often," said The Sarge.

"And you've had this all along?" asked Dave.

Maskell straightened up to face his late best friend's son.

"If he thought I was gonna use it he would have taken it from me the night this happened."

"You mean to say …"

"Yep, he found it. Found it and laughed. Said I could keep it, the cocky little prick."

Once more, Dave drew hope from his friend who only a moment ago seemed to have had all the fight sucked out of him; if he was ready to hurl insults at Norman Layer, then he might just be ready to throw sticks and stones an 'all.

Mick and Danny sat there in disbelief that this man, a policeman no less, had been in possession of a murder confession for over twenty years.

Dave didn't like the idea of running away. "This

whole Cambridge thing … I don't like it," he said. "You've been running all your life, Sarge. You're looking over your shoulder … But you can't even look in the mirror. That's no way for a man to live."

"I don't know what you think you're gonna do instead," said Sarge. "He can't be fought – not by four men."

"I tell you what we're gonna do," said Dave, riled by the phoney justice in his county of birth and the cowardice of the man he once looked up to, "we're gonna put up a *fight*. That's right – we're gonna beat this Norman Layer at his own fucking game."

"You'll be dead by sunrise," said Maskell as he put away the dictaphone that was his one good card against Layer's very full deck.

He walked towards the door, and he didn't look back as he left.

The phone rang.

Dave answered it.

The calm, raspy voice on the other end was unfamiliar to him, but he knew who it belonged to.

"Your friend was right – you should have left well alone. Be seeing you now."

Click.

The others all heard.

"Is it me or are we in deep shit?" said Mick.

Dave didn't respond, as his head was filled with questions of his own. Like how could a policeman lack the moral fibre to stand up and do what was right? How could he let people push him around like this? Did Maskell not see that he was part of the problem?

There was a quiet knock at the door. Dave checked the curtain and saw the figure of Ted Maskell in the streetlight, and assumed he'd been bullied by his conscience into coming back and doing the right thing. Dave opened the door to let him in.

"Blimey," he said. "There's a sight for sore –"

Dave's mouth fell open as his brain assessed the situation, and it only took a second to work out that it wasn't a good one.

Sarge's face was frozen in horror. His hands were cradling his stomach as blood seeped through his fingers, and even in the darkness Dave could see there was a lot of it. His late friend collapsed on him, sending them both crashing to the floor. Dave pushed the body aside and scrambled to his feet upon which he would now have to think very quickly. He got the door shut, threw the chain across and went back to the living room, where he found Danny and Mick looking rattled.

It seemed that Mick was right: they really were in deep shit.

Chapter 28

"We need to get out of here," said Mick, reacting to the untimely death of their friend (who seemed strangely at peace with a deep and bloody hole in him) by stating the bleedin' obvious.

"We're not going anywhere," said Dave.

"Are you out of your fucking mind?" said Mick.

"He's right. These men are cowards – and we don't run from cowards," said Danny somewhat enigmatically.

As well as causing Dave to wonder if Danny was quite the girly toff he'd always assumed he was, his friend's words also put him in mind of his late father, who ultimately taught him two things about tough situations. Dad told him fear was just a voice that needs to be told to shut up if it talked too loudly, and that pain was just something your body uses to remind you you're still alive.

These had been timely words of advice from

'Hunter Papa', a man who played to win but always played fair. And while Dave had lost fights in his time, he'd never backed down from one, and he didn't plan to now.

"Look, Mick, they're gonna find us anyway … And we're a bit old to be playing hide an' seek, ain't we?"

Mick shook his head as much in disbelief as disagreement.

They heard something scraping the front door, and each of them had a bad feeling that someone was about to force an entry.

"Get in the shadows," Danny whispered. "I can deal with this."

He passed the front door and lifted the chain as he went, knowing there was no point in trying to delay the inevitable. He waited for a second or two and heard the crackle of the door frame splintering, and then a 'chink' as the man known as 'Left-Handed' Pete dropped his crowbar.

"Let's 'ave a look at ya, then," 'Left-Handed' Pete

whispered as he crossed the boundary, carelessly leaving the door open as he did so.

He was carrying a German-built pump-action sawn-off, with a tube-shaped silencer on the barrel and his left hand on the trigger. He inched forwards towards the living room to his left. He put his right arm around the doorway in search of a light switch and felt a sudden dull pain across his forearm. Before the pain could fully register with him, he felt a similar blow to his other wrist, which made him drop his gun. He cursed his stupidity as he turned to face his attacker and hopefully beat the shit out of him, but he never got the chance: Danny brought the iron bar up with both hands and brought it down on Pete's left shoulder. 'Left-Handed' Pete was stunned but still standing, and Danny used the crowbar again, this time swinging it in a loop-the-loop fashion in an attempt to take him out at the knees. The iron bar connected again, and Pete buckled, but he wouldn't go down, so Danny went for his lower back, which knocked the wind out of his opponent but still didn't finish the job.

"Feel free to help, you two," said Danny through gritted teeth, as he brought the weapon up for what he hoped would be the last time.

It turned out 'Left-Handed' Pete had the same survival instinct he did, and in spite of the blows he'd taken he was able to bring his right foot up and kick Danny hard in the gut, winding him and in turn loosening his grip on the crowbar. They fought over it for a second or two as 'Left-Handed' Pete tried to wrestle the weapon out of Danny's hands before Mick, who was nearest, picked up the discarded sawn-off and jammed the butt against the head of his would-be killer. He did it with all the force he could muster and then some, and now, finally, the man known as 'Left-Handed' Pete was down and quite possibly dead.

"What do we do now?" asked Mick, his heart

beating so hard he thought it might burst out from his ribcage.

"To start with, we get a look at him," said Dave. "Bring him through."

Dave hit the lights as Mick and Danny dragged the villain into the living room, Danny having already put the chain across the door again.

Their victim – and now he was just that – was out cold, perhaps dreaming of a life in which he'd chosen a more sensible career as a drayman or a haberdasher. He had a pulse and was still breathing, which came as a relief to Mick only because he didn't want to face a manslaughter charge; his conscience was as clear as it should have been.

The sleeping villain was wearing blue suede shoes and drainpipe jeans, which in combo with his silvery quiff suggested he had once danced to Vince Taylor or Johnny Kidd & the Pirates. So he's not all bad then, Dave thought as he started searching him.

His jeans pockets were empty, he had no key ring on his belt, and there was no wallet or keys or phone anywhere in his BSA jacket. There were just a few pieces of paper.

The first sheet was a printout of an image from earlier that day, presumably from the CCTV in that awful 'Leggero's' place, and Dave, Danny and Mick saw a picture of themselves sitting at a table drinking that dreadful tequila-flavoured beer. The next image was a close-up of Danny in the petrol station earlier that day, queuing up to buy the disposable camera. The third had a clear shot of Mick and Dave waiting in Dave's car out on the forecourt.

But it was the fourth picture that gave Dave a start. This was partly because it stirred up bad memories for him, but mainly because he couldn't see how it had come into this man's possession so quickly. It was a police mug shot from the time he'd been arrested, and in the picture he was bleary-eyed, bloody and forlorn.

It seemed Norman Layer's people worked quickly.

Each of the photos had handwritten names and addresses on the reverse, as well as vehicle registration numbers for Dave and Mick, but not for Danny who didn't drive.

As Dave and Danny rifled through the gunman's pockets, Mick went to check Sarge for breathing or a pulse, but there was neither.

In a way, this came as a relief to him since it meant there was no point calling for an ambulance, which would surely bring about involvement from the police, many of whom he now knew worked for Norman Layer. The late Ted Maskell had a set of keys, a mobile phone and a small revolver about his person, all of which Mick pocketed before a loud bang stopped him and froze him on the spot.

"Give me that," said Danny, lower than a whisper.

The noise it makes when someone tries to open a

door that's on a chain is enough to jangle anyone's nerves, but this was nothing compared with the sound that came a second later as a series of kicks took the thing off its hinges. Slouch entered the building, placing a foot on the discarded shotgun that had sealed his friend's fate a moment earlier.

To his right, he saw one of his targets bringing up a revolver, and he passed his 'sawn-off' to his left hand with lightning speed, then used the hand he'd just freed up to catch the much smaller wrist that held the revolver, almost casually throwing the poor kid headfirst in the opposite direction. He even managed to take his gun as he did this, tossing it aside and away from his subjects. Now they were all in place.

Mick got slowly to his feet, making no attempt to charge the big man or to get away.

"Right, you fucking little ponces," Slouch said, teeth bared, aiming his sawn-off at Dave who stood in the middle. "On yer' knees – and don't think about praying 'cos it's too late for that."

He was a tall, muscle-bound giant, sweating underneath a heavy leather jacket, and he would have been no less menacing without the barrel end of a pump-action shotgun three metres from Dave's face.

"Don't do it," was all Dave had to say, never looking away from the big man.

"I said on your fucking knees!" screamed the ageing street thug, kicking the discarded crowbar out of his way.

None of them flinched, and if Danny and Mick were surprised they were still alive, then Dave wasn't.

Dave sensed that Slouch wasn't completely cold-blooded, he wasn't a true psychopath. The first one wouldn't have given it a moment's thought, Dave reckoned, but the fact that he was laid out in front of them possibly dead and they weren't was all the proof Dave needed: Slouch didn't have it in him. Maybe once, but not anymore.

"You're not gonna kill us, mate."

"Shutcha face and –"

Dave talked right over him. "Your friend here is still breathing. He's hurt, but he's not dead. Why don't we get him some help, eh? We're not helping him by standing here playing cops and robbers are we?"

"Shut. Up. And. Get. On. Your. Fucking. Knees," said Slouch through gritted teeth, confirming what Dave had suspected.

Slouch came forward, stroking his trigger as he did so. Now his shotgun barrel was barely a metre from Dave's face, yet none of them budged an inch.

If he'd wanted to push his luck, Dave could have made a knob-based wisecrack about the cylindrical stainless steel muffler that Slouch, like his accomplice, had screwed onto the end of his gun. The tube-shaped accessory was wider than the gun itself and made it a good ten inches longer. Needing extra length and girth – it was rich pickings …

But when you could almost taste the steel and smell the gunpowder, this didn't seem like such a good idea, so Dave decided to play it straight.

"Shooters aren't your style, mate," he said, perhaps pushing his luck just a little.

Slouch was mad as hell; every word the gobby little fucker said was true, and everyone in the room knew it. And nobody knew it more than the thug with a heart that stood before them now.

"All you've got to do is say we got away," said Dave. "If your boss is as bad as they say he is, then you can do a runner yourself. Come on, you don't want to be doing this, do you?"

For what could have been a minute or an hour, Slouch kept his H & K aimed at Dave's forehead, at a distance from which he couldn't possibly miss. Dave was about ninety percent sure that his plan would work and Slouch would give up the weapon, but that still left a ten percent chance that his teeth might come out the back of his head.

And then it was game over. The big man swore as he loosened his grip on his sawn-off, cursing both his conscience for rearing up at a time like this and the gob-shite college boy who had sussed him out so easily. He swore again as he thought of what would become of him now.

"Give it up," said Dave, now seemingly the one in charge. "It's over ... You've done the right thing. Come on, mate, no one else is getting hurt today."

Slouch lowered his weapon, and for a moment a strange peace came over the scene, in spite of the dead policeman in the hall and the half-dead villain on Dave's sofa.

Dave seemed to have earned the trust of the man

who only a moment ago had been aiming a pump-action shotgun at the space between his eyes. Once the gun was lowered, Dave gave Mick the nod, prompting him to lift the heavy vase on the shelf behind them – that contained the late Don Hunter's ashes, no less – and break it on Slouch's head.

"Well," said Dave, "I was never gonna snort 'em anyway."

The peace was disturbed now, thanks to Mick, who decided it was only right to finish what he started, slugging Slouch hard in the guts and setting him up for Danny, who put the big man out cold with a vicious southpaw uppercut.

And then there were two unconscious criminals in Dave's lounge.

Chapter 29

"The last one went in five minutes ago," said Phillip Howlens.

Howlens had parked his BMW in the street outside Dave's house, about thirty yards from his front door. He watched on foot as he talked to his increasingly impatient colleague Shark, who was waiting in the van along with the rest of the troops. They spoke over a two-way radio, as was the standard old-fashioned method in the field.

"You know the drill," said Shark, ending the conversation.

Howlens certainly did know the drill – if more than five minutes went by, leave them to it and meet Shark and co. at the van, parked on London Road about eighty yards from Dave's house, in the other direction from Howlens watchpoint.

Just as Howlens heard the crackle that signalled that

Shark was tired of talking, he saw a chink of light and a brief flurry of movement outside the house belonging to the man he'd expected to be dead by now.

"Chief," he said into the mouthpiece, "just sit tight for a moment."

"We need to find out who else is out there," said Dave. "Danny, be a love and stick your head 'round the door, would you?"

He would have done too if Mick hadn't had a better idea.

The man known to many (but not to them) as 'Left-Handed' Pete would make an excellent dummy in his near-vegetative state. And since he had intended to kill them, they agreed that this was a good idea.

Danny killed the lights, sending the living room and the hallway into near-total darkness. Then he asked Dave to lend him his zippo and held out his hand where Dave's letterbox used to be. He sparked the flint three times, which he was sure would have been enough to engage any gunmen out front. No return shots were fired, and he was satisfied they were clear from this angle. "Front of house in order and lights down," he whispered. "Ready to check peripherals."

They scooped the left-handed bandit up from the floor, Dave taking the right arm, Danny his left and Mick his legs.

"Right then," said Dave, counting them in as usual, "three, two … One!"

The sleeping crook left headfirst, travelling a few feet before landing on the roof of a stationary BMW, thankfully without triggering the cars alarm or enemy fire.

Elvis had left the building.

"Right, we're going out the front – it's quicker, and I reckon it might be safer an 'all," said Dave. He could be decisive in these situations, and though Danny and Mick thought the garden wall seemed like the safest bet, they had come to trust his judgement.

"Mick?" said Dave.

"Yes, mate?"

"That gun you took off the Sarge – have you ever fired one before?"

"No, Dave."

"Well, you never know your luck. Oh, and the police might wanna use his dictaphone."

"Can't they just dial with their fingers," said Mick, and Dave would have been disappointed if he hadn't.

Dave watched the door as he rallied his men, despite being quietly confident that they were on their own – for now, anyway.

"What about you, Danny? Ever fired a g ..." He turned as he spoke and saw Danny with a shotgun slung over his shoulder. "Mind me chandeliers," he said with a nod and a wink, now convinced that there was more to

Danny than he'd imagined.

"What about him?" asked Danny, looking down at the other semi-conscious villain who hadn't left the building.

"What ... Old Slouch here?" said Dave, making Slouch stir a little when he heard his name. "He's more use to us here, what with the gun and the prints an' all."

"He's coming round, lads," said Mick, who was the first to notice.

The butt of Danny's shotgun put a stop to that, and they made their exit.

"I dunno how they did it, but they've taken care of Pete, and Slouch is still inside."

"Whaddaya mean they've 'taken care' of him?" demanded Shark.

"One of them must have thrown a lucky punch or something, because 'Left-Handed' Pete's out cold."

The other two in the van heard all this and perked up a little – maybe they'd see some action tonight after all.

"They're out the house and heading away."

Howlens was crouching behind a parked car as he had this conversation and used his night-vision 'bins' to monitor the targets.

"They've gone down a side-street, and I've just heard car doors closing."

There was a pause as Howlens had a quick look around for any curious bystanders or witnesses; Shark wondered why Howlens couldn't just go in and finish them himself, but he would soon find out.

"Okay, vehicle now moving south and heading towards London Road. You should see 'em any minute."

A few seconds later, his radio crackled.

"Got 'em," said Shark.

Howlens shivered at the way his colleague relayed this information. He knew that 'got 'em' meant that Shark had seen his target, but before the night was out it would mean something quite different.

"Oh, and they've got Pete's gun by the look of it," he said.

Adrenaline and the thrill of the chase sometimes blunts the senses. They can also blunt people's good sense, something now evinced by Danny, who was grinning as he walked the streets of Colchester with a pump-action shotgun resting on his shoulder.

Mick raised his hand to alert Dave to Danny's rookie/schoolboy error, but Dave just gave him a wink as if to say 'let him get it out of his system.' It was only a short walk to the car and a good hour from the kicking-out time at The Lion, so all seemed well.

Not that all was quite as well as it seemed, of course. Dave knew it, and Danny did too.

While Mick was looking out for passersby, it hadn't

escaped the notice of the other two that they were being watched. As they'd started walking towards their getaway vehicle, out of the corner of his eye, Danny had seen the faintest reflection of streetlight on glass in the shadow of the old cemetery wall across the street, about thirty yards down. Their observer had made good use of the cover that darkness provides, but not great use of it. Danny looked at Dave, who nodded to confirm that he too had seen it.

They'd kept walking, and both men reasoned inwardly that if they'd got this far out in the open without being sprayed with bullets, then it was likely their spy was unarmed.

In spite of their bravado, they were relieved to make it to the car and comforted by the fact that they would soon be away from all this. Where they were going, of course, only one of them knew.

"He'll know what direction we're going in," said Danny from the back seat, happy to let Mick ride shotgun now that *he* was holding one.

"Who will?" asked Mick, confused and also rather irked at being kept in the dark just like the person who was watching them.

"We were being watched back there – some geezer in the distance had a pair of binoculars," said Dave. "I didn't tell you cos I didn't want to worry you."

Danny laughed, but never took his eyes off the target.

"Us real soldiers, eh Danny?" said Dave.

Danny didn't reply, and if the other two didn't know better, they'd have sworn he was willing whoever was watching them to come out from the shadows and try something.

Chapter 30

"That'll be them, then," said Dave as the headlights lit up and the Mercedes van swung out into London Road behind them.

The van's driver may have been unconcerned about masking his intentions, at least not to Dave and co., but thankfully he didn't give his lackeys orders to fire. He was a safe and careful driver, and Dave was surprised he hadn't tried to run his Impreza off the road or turn this into a high-speed pursuit – at least not yet.

It's coming, though – sure as you're born it is ...

Having turned left, Dave drove along Colchester's Avenue of Remembrance, heading east at a steady 40 making regular mirror checks – something he didn't bother with much on a normal drive, reasoning that you had to stop whenever you had to stop. If someone's too close, they're going to hit you whether you see it coming or not, so why spoil the surprise?

Casual observers might not have known he was doing the exact opposite of what he appeared to be doing; he was taking care *not* to lose the black van and the people in it.

He had plans for them, had done for a while – long before they came to his street and gunned his friend down right on his doorstep. His plans were sketchy at the moment, but he was sure of one thing: either these fuckers were going down, or they were going somewhere where it wasn't a good idea to drop your shower cap too often.

"Come to papa," he whispered, as he checked his rear for the seventeenth time in half a mile.

"Where are we going, Dave?"

It was Mick who asked, though both he and Danny were curious.

"You heard the Sarge. This Norman Layer's got half the county in his back pocket so that rules out involving Essex Police altogether."

"Suffolk?" Mick suggested.

"Too close," said Dave. "He'll have people there an' all."

Silence fell as Mick and Danny considered their seemingly limited options.

"I think our only hope is to try and find this friend of his in Cambridge," said Danny.

Dave and Mick nodded approval at their friend's suggestion.

"You've got Sarge's phone, Mick?"

"Right here, chief," Mick said, tapping the left-breast pocket of his blue denim jacket. "See if you can find a Cambridge number. Hopefully, this Burnham fella's got more bottle than The Sarge."

While Mick and Dave plotted, back in Southend Norman Layer was starting to lose his cool, even though this was something he usually considered foolish. For a time he paced the floor of the clubhouse office like a lion in a cage, almost sick with rage at these college boys who wanted to poke their noses into his business and thought they could take him on. He wasn't used to this, and he didn't like it one little bit.

Though neither party knew it, this was an indicator of the fight going away from Layer's favour; a chess player knows that in a battle of wills the steadiest hand usually belongs to the victor.

His phone rang, and he answered before the second ring.

"Are they dead yet?" Layer listened for a moment as Shark tried to explain the situation. "Then why the fuck are you blabbering down the phone to me?"

For about ten seconds, Norman Layer shook his head in disbelief at what he was hearing. Then he grew tired of Shark's excuses and shut him up by talking right over him. "Don't call this number again until those college boys have stopped breathing. Understand?"

He hung up before his employee could answer then sat down, realising that losing his cool would mean losing his focus. And that was not going to help him win the day. He took a cigar and tapped it on his desk a few times, before deciding against it and sliding it back in the box. These were for relaxation, and this was no time for that.

He wondered just how the hell these three supposedly easy targets had not only got away but had somehow managed to disarm and incapacitate two of his best men. Had he underestimated his opponents?

By now, their bodies should be cooling on the way to the morgue.

Then the answer came to him: he'd do it himself, and in the morning he'd sort out his staffing problems.

He mumbled darkly as he opened his safe and fetched his revolver – something about college boys who don't know they're born, and how they'd pray for death before it came.

"Bingo!" said Mick, forgetting for a moment that the car's windows could explode at any second.

His announcement came as Dave went from 40mph to the national speed limit, careful not to outrun the van – which he could easily do – but taking even greater care not to let it get within his very roughly estimated shooting range.

"What y' got mate?"

"Robert Burnham. Both his home number his and work number begin zero-one-two-two-three."

"Sterling work, old boy. Now give me the phone and take the wheel. Good lad."

Mick leaned across and took the wheel as Dave put in a call to this Burnham chap who would soon be out of retirement and his dressing gown.

He took it rather well.

It was just before ten when the phone rang, and Mr and Mrs Burnham were finishing their cocoa and getting ready for bed.

They were not used to being disturbed at this time of night and hadn't been since Mr Burnham left the force two years earlier and they'd moved out of town to a lovely village in rural Cambridgeshire.

Nothing much happened before sundown in sleepy Felston, Cambridgeshire, population just over five-hundred, and even less happened after. You had a few ruddy-faced locals making their way back from The Plough after last orders, but these were likeable old souls who were never too unruly. On Christmas Eve a few people made their way to and from midnight mass, but there was never any aggro, in spite of the free wine. Well, only once or twice.

In fact, Robert and his lovely wife Yvonne often

remarked to guests that the reason it was safe to walk the streets around here after dark was that nobody did.

As he took the call, his wife gave him a look of concern and disapproval.

"Yes, this is he, Robbie Burnham. Who is this please? I see. Yes, Sergeant Maskell is a friend of mine. How is he by the way? Oh, I see … He's dead, is he?"

The conversation went on like this for some time. Initially, Robert Burnham suspected this was a rather distasteful prank until the mention of a certain name seemed to get his attention. His wife was about to turn and go to bed, but Burnham cupped the receiver and called to her to stop.

"Get me a notepad would you, dear – I need to write a few things down."

Their journey continued into the night, and Dave was thankful he'd filled his tank back at the garage where

Danny had bought the plastic camera. Dave had done some miles today, but there was enough left in the tank to make it to Cambridge.

They were near Ipswich by the time he'd finished relaying the story to the late Sarge's friend Robbie Burnham. The sloping, hilly sections of the A12 provided a natural shield from any target practice from Layer's men, as Dave was careful not to lose their pursuers. He checked regularly that he could see headlights pointed skywards behind every slope in the road, knowing that if he could see them, then they could see him.

Dave updated them as they passed the Toys 'R Us roundabout' and joined the Cambridge-bound A14. "Bob Burnham's told us to meet him at Cambridge city centre police station, and that he'd call his old skipper in the meantime."

"How long's that going to take us?" asked Danny, not familiar with the area.

"Well," said Dave, "it's sixty miles to Cambridge. I've got a full tank of gas, half a pack of cigarettes, it's dark, and we're wearing sunglasses."

They all laughed for the first time in a while.

One thing Dave had noticed was that this Burnham chap had seemed rather less than cut up over the death of his late friend and colleague. And while this seemed strange at first, he realised that he too was mostly unmoved by the man's passing, and it wasn't because The Sarge hadn't been the man he'd thought he was. Given his friend's lot in life, Dave could see that Ted Maskell was actually better off dead. Dave Hunter, wise beyond his years and smarter than many or most, knew that a life not worth living was just that.

Dave could see that, like the people who brought the blues to America and got the whole thing started, Ted Maskell had lived his life within strict boundaries, his freedom taken from him. Now that he was dead, he no longer answered to anybody.

"So what happens when we get to Cambridge?" asked Danny, as the miles clocked up.

"Well, old bean, we won't be going to look at any museums or cathedrals," said Dave. "Let's just say the Cambridge Constabulary take a dim view of people bringing guns onto their patch."

"Good job it's not here," said Mick as he saw the sign for Stowmarket and their surroundings became more rural. "All they'd have to do is say they're shooting pigeons."

Chapter 31

The late Don Hunter had been a film enthusiast, and for this reason, Dave was well acquainted with movies from what many consider to be the golden age of cinema. His father having been a particular fan of the late Steve McQueen, Dave saw a great many high-speed chases ride out across their rental TV as a lad. He'd liked them too, reckoned they were dead exciting.

Not so the real thing, he realised as his game of cat and mouse trundled on across Suffolk. He was grimly aware of course that being remote and very dark an'all, this would make an ideal spot for murder.

But he didn't give it too much thought, and he could only reason that his cool detachment was a deep-seated fight-or-flight response to the situation at hand. What he didn't realise was that he was pondering the absurdity of experiencing boredom while being 'pursued' by assassins only because his brain had told him to. The instruction to do this came from the same part of his brain that generated the survival instinct that had allowed him to keep his friends and himself alive against such seemingly high odds, and he probably didn't realise that, either.

In other words, it was a reminder for him to keep his game up.

"Are we nearly there yet?" asked Mick as he lit his third cigarette of the journey.

"Sit tight, mate – you can have a kip on my knee if you want," was the best response that Dave could manage.

Though they had made many late-night gig returns together before, it was unusual for Dave to be driving. Usually, he sat front-centre in Mick's works van, swigging from a bottle while Danny snoozed next to him.

Tonight, Danny had been quiet most of the way, but he definitely wasn't sleeping; several times the other two had looked back suspecting that the rhythms of the road had lulled him into slumber, but no. He was poised like a panther, ready to spring – to *kill* – at a second's notice.

They sped past Newmarket. Despite the circumstances that had brought him this way, Dave found himself wondering, as he always did when he came through here, what it must be like to play Newmarket Racecourse. He'd heard they could hold 20,000 at their summer concerts there; that would suit him, thank you very much, even though he'd probably blow most of his fee on the horses.

He knew that they would soon see the 'Welcome to Cambridge' sign. He also knew exactly where the exit was, having made this journey many times before. In fact, he knew every lay-by and Little Chef in the south of England, such was the musician's way of life.

Then everything went dark – really dark – which seemed strange since the sun went down four hours ago.

It happened the moment that they passed the sign

for the change of county, or the 'city limits' as the Yanks called it. The sodium lights above the carriageway went out, and it was hard to tell how far back the darkness stretched. It could have been a whole mile, and the Mercedes van behind them was also in the mysterious black zone.

It was the same story ahead of them: there really was no light at the end of the tunnel.

Dave's mind raced. As he saw it, one of two things had happened. Either the people out here in the countryside had decided they didn't like this new-fangled *'lectricity* after all, or the Cambridgeshire Highways Agency had also been infiltrated by Norman Layer. It put Dave in mind of that spooky old Charlie Musselwhite song *My Road Ahead Lies in Darkness*.

It also reminded him of a troubling dream he'd had a few times, in which he'd be driving at night along a familiar route only to find himself in a supermarket car park. The supermarket was always closed in the dream, the car park was free of cars, and there were no shoppers, just a dozen or so faceless vagrants with unkempt Alsatians, and Dave would notice his headlight beam dimming and failing to cut through the darkness.

Sensing the end was nigh, he decided he would floor it and make one last push for survival – it wasn't like he could turn back now. He hit 80mph and left the black van for dust, but he didn't keep this speed up for long.

In fact, he didn't even put another mile on the clock.

In the distance, about a quarter of a mile away stood the silhouetted figure of a man with his feet straddling the two-lane carriageway. He was wearing a black hat, which matched the rest of his attire and looked to Dave like a trilby or fedora but was actually a beekeeper's hat. He held out his hand, motioning for Dave to slow down.

As they got closer to him, Dave felt he saw something kindly in the older man; he seemed trustworthy and honest, so Dave ceded to his request to stop. Dave stopped the car at his feet and wound down his window as the mystery man walked around to his side.

"You're alright now. You're with us," was all he said, tapping Dave's door, and all three of them believed him for he spoke with warmth and reassurance.

Robert Burnham, 64

Always very much a grassroots copper, Robbie Burnham had never been interested in the pen-pushing and political correctness that would surely have come with promotion. He saw no shame in taking orders if you believed in what you were doing. The only shame lay in not carrying out an order properly, for if a job was worth doing, then Mr Burnham believed it was worth it doing well.

He'd been a good friend of the late Sergeant Maskell, but they had been in contact less frequently since Burnham left for Cambridgeshire ten years ago, planning to see out his remaining two years of work before settling into cosy rural retirement.

Neither short nor tall, Burnham had an air of authority about him, but he also possessed a fundamental decency which he didn't let people abuse. He had common sense, and throughout his working life, Burnham firmly believed that helping someone in trouble was a better way to use his time than writing tickets for somebody he'd seen driving at 32 miles per hour.

Shark wanted to lean out the passenger side window and put some holes in the car ahead and hopefully its occupants, but his driver, Ron Butler, wouldn't allow it.

Shark resented being told what to do by a mere driver, but even he knew protocol: when the vehicle was moving, the driver was in charge. So Shark sat sulking in the back of the van, banging the back of his head against his headrest and stroking his fingers over the steel, teeth-like ridges in the frame of his Heckler & Koch.

Naturally, this made the other people in the back of the van want to keep half an eye on him. He was a caged animal, a bear with a sore head – something he would have for real if he didn't stop banging it like that.

Or, as at least one of them back there had thought, if he doesn't stop acting like a c**t.

None of this made life very pleasant for Mr Ron Butler, who had to drive the van knowing he had an angry psychopath with a deadly firearm aboard, not wearing his seatbelt or making any effort to play nicely with the other boys. He knew he should tell Shark to behave himself, to wind it in and be professional like the rest, but he didn't want to chance it.

Then the carriageway went pitch black, and he wondered what the fuck was happening.

"You just sit and watch the show, alright?"

As the words left Bob Burnham's lips, a long line of police cars – a dozen or more, each with no lights and driving the wrong way down the carriageway – came up and formed a roadblock just yards ahead of Dave's stationary Impreza. Then six vanloads of armed response officers from the Cambridgeshire constabulary arrived, and their drivers got them into position.

"All a bit exciting, isn't it?" said Mick, glad to be at a place of safety but not showing his relief.

They were underneath a motorway bridge, and a rumbling overhead announced the arrival of the second cavalry.

Once the vehicles were all in place, police officers hurried to get two-thousand-watt portable floodlights in position on the roof of their squad cars, all pointing in the direction of the fast-approaching Mercedes van. The firearms unit spread out and scrambled into position; some crouched behind vehicles, others found cover by the roadside. Either way, they all knew what they were doing.

A senior-ranking firearms officer switched on his megaphone and began the hard part – the waiting, knowing that at least it wouldn't be for long.

If things going dark had taken Ron Butler by surprise, then it was nothing compared to seeing the night sky light up like Las Vegas less than a minute later. Butler put up his right arm to shield his eyes, instinctively keeping one hand on the wheel as he slowed the van to a halt and bought it to rest some way from the roadblock. He couldn't cross the central reservation, so he made a desperate turn in the road, going for his only hope, even though his chances of making it back to Essex the wrong way down a dual-carriageway were slim at best.

He made the manoeuvre but was stopped by another blinding light from the direction he was now facing; the Suffolk constabulary had been informed and had also acted quickly. More flashing blues, more floodlights, more armed police. The hunter was now well and truly the hunted and about to become the catch. Butler yelled an obscenity as the van stopped moving.

For a moment there was silence, as the chief firearms officer was yet to make contact. He knew, and all his officers knew that if shots were to be fired, as seemed likely, then it was best to let the team members' eyes adjust to the transition from dark to dazzling albeit only briefly.

Everything was in place, but he'd learned over a long and varied career that it was best to let things settle since his goal was to try to resolve the situation *without* shots being fired.

The Mercedes van sat idle, and Ron Butler was the first one to accept his fate and come out with his hands up. For a moment he stood completely still with his breath clouded in the blue illuminations until he was told via a stern blast of a megaphone to lay face down, arms and legs apart and fully stretched out.

Then there was a loud bang as the back door of the Mercedes van flew open and the man known as Shark leapt out with his gun raised, having decided death was better than prison and better still if he took a few coppers with him.

It never came to pass, and the loud bang Shark's DM boot made against the back door of the van was followed by another one from an assault rifle held by 'Number One' (real name Greg Ridley) of the quickly assembled unit. At 21, he was an expert marksman, and he knew he'd be the first one to fire. He went for the headshot and got it, catching the big brute right between the eyes and destroying the troubled brain that powered them.

At least one officer on the Suffolk side openly cursed the Cambridge lot for getting the first shot, but they never had the chance to make it one-all: the remaining bad guys came quietly and did as they were told.

Ron Butler got up and made a run for it, natch, correctly assuming that no policeman would shoot an unarmed man, but he was soon caught in a nearby field. He was taken down by a big lad named Arthur McMullen, a volunteer who worked the fields around here by day, seizing both his chance and the villain at the same time. There was no need for any rough stuff, but there was no need for Mr Butler to call him a 'fucking carrot-cruncher' either, so he used a little bit more force than necessary to apprehend him – just a little bit more, mind.

Chapter 32

"Bravo!" said the Chief Constable, his words hurtling down the line and into the Chief Superintendent's tinny earpiece. "Sterling work, old chap. Can't have these bloody –"

His voice went quiet as the Chief Superintendent turned the volume down to speak to the three shivering and exhausted Essex lads, now waiting in a patrol car, drinking tea and watching their breath rise in the blue lights flashing around them. Mick wondered if they'd be given blankets like in the movies; they all wondered if they could have something stronger than tea to drink, but nobody wanted to be the one to ask.

They were allowed to smoke though, and at least that was something. There was no chance of them going home tonight, as they would need to assist the local constabulary with their investigation, provide statements etc., so the authorities would have to put them up in a hotel where, if there was a God after all, the bar would still be open.

The 'Chief Super' leaned in through the squad car's front window. He looked upset about something, and it wasn't being whisked away from his annual bowls club Committee And Secretaries Dinner – although that was an important local fixture.

"I don't think much of you bringing these bloody hoodlums into our county," he said to Dave, having selected him as ambassador. "Not really our thing, you see. We have a peaceful way of life out here near the Fens, and our criminals seem to respect that."

He paused, perhaps reprimanding himself for being harsh with them so hastily. "The Chief Constable's over the moon of course, but he didn't have to come down here and deal with it did he, eh?" The Super shook his head, saddened by what he saw and the modern world in general.

"He'll most probably get to meet the Queen over a

big job like t…"

"What's the matter, Chief?" Dave asked him, wondering what had stopped him in his tracks, but then he noticed a smile creeping onto his face and he knew the Super was up to something.

The Chief Super had just remembered that he too was in the business of chasing promotion, and he seriously doubted that the two men he was up against had ever been involved with something as high-profile as this. Also, the Chief Constable was retiring next month …

"In just a moment we're going to take you to a Holiday Inn a few miles away. No doubt you'll need refreshment, so I'll put some money behind the bar for you. I would join you only I'll be here all night with this 'orrible lot."

It was hard to know if he meant the criminals or the members of the Suffolk constabulary who had been involved in the joint sting, but Dave, like his two friends, simply didn't care. There would be cool draughts at the hotel, and he wanted one of those like a blind man wanted to paint the things he saw in his dreams.

They were taken by police escort to a nearby Holiday Inn, where their new friend Bob Burnham joined them for a few drinks.

As they drained several cold Buds (it wasn't even worth asking if they did Estuary Lager this far from civilisation) in the dimly lit hotel bar, Burnham explained a few things.

He told them he was a good friend of Terence Staple, Chief Constable of Cambridgeshire Police, and that he and his wife Yvonne regularly had dinner with the CC and his wife, Diane. Because of this, and Maskell's reputation for excellence in the local constabulary, he knew he could always have the Chief Constable's ear (without grovelling like many shamelessly did in the company of influential people).

Burnham had put the phone down directly after Dave had called him earlier that evening. Then he called Staple at home and told him what going down, thus setting in motion the build-up to the grand finale that had just played out right before their eyes on the Suffolk/Cambridge border.

Burnham explained that he, along with Staple and the Chief Superintendent they'd met earlier, had quickly rallied a forty-strong team to man the roadblock on the Cambridge side and a similar detachment on the Suffolk side. Every entrance to the West Bound A14 was blocked by officers from the Suffolk traffic division, and every vehicle that was already on the carriageway was stopped by blue lights and taken to the nearest exit or slip road. Each squad manning the exits radioed the next stop along when Dave's vehicle and the trailing black Mercedes van passed until they were both in the 'trap zone'. The word of the

Chief Constable was enough to get a senior employee from the Highways Agency primed to kill the overhead lights when the signal was given. And that, one minor detail withstanding, was that.

"We received an anonymous tip-off that another vehicle was coming for you. We've not found it yet, but the traffic lot are on to it now. We've got the registration, so it shouldn't take long, but you'll have to stay here till the dust settles."

"How long will that be?" asked Dave, who was as entranced by the headlights rushing along the nearby M11 as he was by this remarkable story.

"Could be a while," said Burnham. "The fine old county of Essex is in a right old 'two and eight' by the look of things," he said before looking up at Mick for some reason. "I knew I shouldn't have left. Norman Layer and everyone who works for him will need rounding up, but it will be hard – correction, nigh-on bloody impossible – with so many people in the job working for him. Suffice to say the county you go back to could be rather different from the one you left."

He turned to walk out into the night but stopped and turned to face them all once more.

"They'll be recruiting once this is all over – you could join up. We'll need brave young lads like you – even old 'girly' here might get in if he gets his hair cut."

This comment went unnoticed by Danny who was nursing a beer and still upset about being forced to give up his gun.

An impressive collection of empties formed over the next couple of hours and the conversation flowed as did the drink while the ashtrays filled. One topic that two of the party, Mick and Dave, eventually got around to was Daniel Blyth – or more to the point, Daniel Blyth and his secret inner *badass*. They all fared well throughout their adventure, but Danny had known just what to do at crucial moments; he knew how to hold a gun, and he'd looked like he was ready to use it, too.

Danny told Mick and Dave that he started playing the piano at an early age, and it had been a source of much joy for him. But his strict, troubled father had not approved of Danny's preoccupation with music or more specifically the piano.

This wasn't strictly true, but it was partly true, and anybody who knew the truth would not have blamed Danny for bending it in this way for, in fact, Peter Blyth had noticed that his youngest son Daniel had adopted a pet toy the way children sometimes do.

In Danny's case, tragically – or hilariously – it was one of his sister Violet's My Little Pony dolls. And, while this was probably harmless enough, his father hadn't seen it that way, interpreting it instead as some kind of cry for help.

So at the age of seven, Daniel Blyth became the

world's first aspiring concert pianist to take up boxing since Billy Joel. For years and years, Danny went to that damned gymnasium, where he was like a fish out of water. But like anyone dumped outside of their comfort zone for any period, he adapted; he learned to get by and eventually came to thrive in this environment. Not that this was enough for his father, of course, and Danny found himself locked in a steely battle of wills with him; Danny refused to give up playing the expensive Steinway in the Blyth reading room (purchased purely for decorative purposes), so the punishments intensified. The school rugby club. The weekend survivalist camps. The army cadets. And finally, the clincher.

Danny's older brother, Miles, had done the right thing in their father's eyes, treating university only as a stepping stone towards officer training in the British army, and in doing so making the old boy proud. Danny, by contrast, had always made it clear that his plans were different, which had never gone down well with his father (his mother had little say in anything on their estate other than what to buy the maid for Christmas).

With his youngest son's coming-of-age imminent, Danny's father issued an ultimatum: if Danny wanted to study music, he would have to join the army as a boy soldier first. If he didn't at the very least complete basic training, then he could pay his own way through university. And if he didn't like that he could find somewhere else to live.

As it happens, he did grow to like it, and he completed his training admirably just around the time that 'bloody business in Afghanistan' flared up. Danny didn't detail the horrors he'd seen on his tours of the wretched place, and he didn't need to.

"Bloody hell," said Mick. "Couldn't he have just changed your name to Sue and been done with it."

Dave shook his head in disbelief at what he was

hearing. It's another world, he thought as he stared out at

the two-lane carriageway, now as quiet and as dark as the

grave.

Chapter 33

Dave woke up in the back of a car.

It was hard to say which car or whose it was since he was blindfolded and gagged with what he suspected was duct tape. His hands were cuffed behind his back.

His mind raced, but he drew a blank as to where he was or how he'd got there. One minute he was dozing in the hotel bar after one too many with Mick and Danny, and now … This?

He didn't know where Danny or Mick were, but he sensed neither was the person next to him jabbing a barrel into his rib cage. He decided not to say anything.

After a while (it was hard to say how long) the car came to a stop. "Let's move," said the person next to him before dragging him out of the car. Dave had a dizzy spell and nearly fell to the floor, but his captor steadied him and kept him upright using both hands, meaning his gun was strapped to him, Dave thought.

They walked a few steps before the man who had just held him upright threw him to the floor. Dave found himself being dragged up an outdoor fire escape face down and arms first, scraping his knees and shins on the corrugated iron steps as they went. At the top of the stairwell he was dragged indoors, and he heard a heavy steel door closing behind him. He was pulled a few feet inside the building and dumped in a heap on the brown carpeted floor.

His blindfold was ripped off (fuck, that hurt) and he saw he was in what must have been a warehouse office, a sparse affair overlooking the shop-floor, which Dave imagined was dingy and soulless after being stripped of its machinery. It wasn't hard to know who was sat at the desk in front of him, brandishing a pistol, but there was an enamelled gold plaque in case he needed it spelling out to him:

It was hard to make out his face in the dimly lit room, but from what Dave could see Layer looked like just he had imagined, granite-jawed and cold-eyed, with a long, bony face.

"You really should learn to mind your own business."

This was followed by a bright light and a deafening crack, and after that the room went very dark indeed.

Dave woke with a start then shook off the dream that had disrupted his slumber; he now knew that real life could be just as scary. He walked down the stairs and into the hotel lobby, where his two friends were waiting in company with several police officers including the ambitious Chief Superintendent they had met last night.

Dave didn't say anything; he just lit a cigarette and

prepared for a long period of questioning, deciding there and then that he would take a holiday when this was all over.

Outside, it was one of those disappointing spring mornings that were colder than they looked and neither sunny or grey. Dave was concerned that the police hadn't returned his car yet and flummoxed as to why they wanted it in the first place – didn't they trust him to stay put?

He was also conscious of having the potentially incriminating dictaphone about his person; he hadn't wanted to be separated from it and had made the decision not to leave it in his car. He planned to show it at a time of his choosing, aware that this could have the effect of rendering it unusable as evidence.

As he was thinking about this, and the police officers were shooting the breeze in the hotel car park, a silver Jaguar carrying a licence plate that read N LAYER 1 came to a steady halt near the car park entrance. Had it been speeding then it may have caught the police officers' attention, but Norman Layer was too clever for that, and his arrival escaped the notice of all except for one: Daniel Peter Blyth.

The electronic window wound itself halfway down, and the barrel took aim at Dave. Danny reacted instantly, slamming his friend to the ground and shielding him from the shots fired, taking several in the back himself.

There were twelve officers in total, and most took cover when shots rang out; many hit the deck, others dived behind stationary squad cars. Some, however, were unsure how to respond and simply froze.

Three of the officers on the scene – the ones who instinctively took cover behind vehicles – were firearms officers. They drew their weapons quickly, but Layer was faster still, and by the time they'd taken aim he'd made good his escape and almost reached 60mph.

Dave, somehow resisting the need to go into shock, eased his friend down, not knowing if you were meant to move a gunshot victim at all let alone one who'd been hit in the back. Mick rushed over, and for a time they held their friend and prayed silently.

Then Dave realised that praying wasn't all he could do. It was Bond vs Blofeld, and he decided that Bond had better get a blooming move on.

One of the officers had been standing with his keyring over the aerial of his radio that was clipped to his stab-protection jacket. The policeman had been too shocked to really notice his keyring come loose as he'd hit the deck, and now it was sitting before Dave, just a few feet away.

This is my only chance, Dave thought as he grabbed the keys and got in the squad car that blocked the entrance to the car park; Norman Layer was going to pay.

And with that he began his second three-county car chase in one day, only this time he was the hunter – Dave

Hunter.

As he pursued the silver car onto the Suffolk-bound A14, it occurred to Dave that when he'd gone after the bad guy, Danny was smiling. This seemed strange to Dave, who had always thought that death must be very bad indeed.

He remembered when, a couple of years ago, he'd found out that The Who's Jon Entwistle had died. That night, as Dave and a few of the lads raised a glass in the taproom snug, one of the mourners had comforted his friends with the fact that the ex-bass guitarist must've died with a smile on his face since he had been found with a body full of cocaine and a bed full of hookers. Then, Dave Hunter understood.

Danny was at peace because he'd taken a bullet for a friend: his honour had been restored after legging it on the night of the Irish wedding in Thurrock.

That silly bastard.

The chase continued into Suffolk, past Newmarket and Stowmarket, with both Dave and his target changing lanes like Britain changes its weather. Dave kept right on his tail as they weaved in and out of traffic, not sure how this would end, only sure that Norman Layer's life would end.

As they left Ipswich and got back on the A12, it occurred to Dave that Layer was doing something he had considered most unlikely: he was going back to Essex. Dave realised that it was only the distance involved that made this seem like such an audacious move; once Layer was back in the county he part-owned then, in theory, he would be safe.

Which was more than could be said for me, Dave thought as he passed the 'Welcome to Essex' sign. The county's three-seax coat of arms brought Slouch to mind, and the collection of lethal weaponry they had seen in his home only yesterday – and the fact that Slouch was, as far as Dave knew, still unaccounted for.

Still out there, and most likely mad as hell at Dave Hunter.

Don't think about that now, Dave thought as he drove, noticing the sun had come out around the time they crossed the county line.

***

They passed the turn-off for Chelmsford roughly 30 minutes later, and now Dave realised what was going on: Norman Layer thought he was going to escape to sea.

He was planning to travel along the estuary and sail off into the sunset and live happily ever after in a country with an agreeable climate and a relaxed attitude towards extradition and international banking laws.

Not on my watch …

They left the A12 at Junction 17 and tore across towards

the oil city, where Norman Layer's speedboat and a suitcase full of used notes was waiting for him. It was going so well for Dave, right up until the moment when Layer decided to ignore a red light at a busy junction just beyond Canvey Way. Nothing wrong with that, Dave thought as he prepared to do the same, only it was hard to argue with the heavy goods lorry coming across, or the bus behind it or the team of cyclists that followed that. Don't do it, he thought, even if the BMX bandits were about to spare the life of a man for whom prison really was too good.

He didn't do it, but he did hurl an insult and make the accompanying gesture, which must have seemed strange coming from a police car.

It was only as Dave slipped back into gear after his run-in with the local cycling proficiency team that he noticed that his dashboard was lighting up like Guy Fawkes Night. Blue LEDs flashed madly. Green, yellow, red … Something was going down somewhere, and someone thought it was something big. Dave turned the volume up a little, and amidst the white noise and hysteria he was able to pick out something about a stolen car. Which seemed a tad trifling, all things considered.

Dave lowered the volume, shutting out this unnecessary distraction from the important job of catching and killing Norman Layer. Layer had lost him for now, but Dave knew where he was going, and now it was just a matter of time.

He passed the sign for Canvey Jetty, not that he needed it: he knew exactly where this was.

He followed the winding, gravelly road through the sand dunes up to where the boats were moored, and two things caught his eye. First, he saw Norman Layer speeding along the estuary in a Monterey Super Sport – a very sleek, very expensive and very fast high-performance speedboat. Then, he saw the man with the rockabilly quiff from last night, standing only metres in front of Dave's bonnet and pointing a revolver in his direction.

This did nothing to slow the progress of the car driven by a man who was driven by revenge. 'Left-Handed' Pete cocked the revolver, aimed, and fired. Dave's windscreen made an almighty noise as it shattered, but the bullet missed him, so he drove on. Pete fired again and missed again, and still, Dave drove. 'Left-Handed' Pete chambered a new round then aimed and fired once more. This time he caught Dave on his left side, just beneath his collarbone, but it was a mere flesh wound and Dave, gripping the wheel and gritting his teeth in determination, drove on. He had him now.

Pete's body made a sickening thud as it bounced across the bonnet, and Dave saw the whites of the dead man's eyes, his body impaled in grizzly fashion by the remains of the car's windscreen, and whose head was hanging where the passenger's lap would have been.

"That's for Ted Maskell, you fucking pansy."

And now one for Danny. This would require expert timing, Dave thought – timing and tactics.

Ahead of him, there was a long wooden jetty that stood about six feet above the water and projected maybe twenty feet into it. The only people who used this were the local winos at night, meaning it was clear as Dave needed it to be. Keeping his speed up and hoping the simple wooden structure didn't collapse beneath him, Dave sped towards the end of the small pier, where he turned the wooden safety rail to splinters. The RPM counter hit the red, and the engine roared as the tyres lost traction on the ground. The vehicle cleared fifty feet before landing on top of Norman Layer's speedboat and on top of Norman Layer, crushing the cockpit and killing him instantly.

The cruiser slowed to a halt, unable to reach its impressive speed with a Ford Focus parked on it, and its once-noisy inboard engine no longer roared – it purred idly and pathetically; the boat was history, and so was its owner.

This was all watched by a crew of whiskery old sea dogs, returning from a slow and dispiriting trawl. They'd been disappointed with their catch that morning, but that mattered no more, for they each had a tale to tell down at The Mariners Inn tonight.

And tomorrow night, and probably the one after that too.

Dave was giddy from the impact. In fact, he was concussed and completely delirious, but he was unharmed save for some bleeding from his upper body where the bullet had somehow passed right through him. He was disappointed he forgot to yell "Yippee-ki-yay, motherfuckers!" as the car left the ground, but he could say he did next time he was in The Red Lion, and that was all that mattered; he knew you didn't let the truth get in the way of a good story.

He lifted the handset on the radio and pushed the intercom, making a 'ksssch' sound as he did it.

"The situation's under control," he said with a raspy snigger, as he realised the boat – and therefore the car – was sinking into the estuary. Fuck it, he thought. The coastguard will be along soon.

Dave looked across at the cadaver that was half in and half out of the stolen police car and wondered why he wasn't more troubled by its presence. Then, he spotted a megaphone in the passenger foot space, presumably left there from the night before, which he picked up then held to his mouth. "Come in number six, your time is up!" he said over the 'tannoy' while pinching his nose before he started to laugh so hard he was surprised he didn't pass out.

Then he did.

Epilogue

It was a busy summer in the county of Essex that year. More than two-hundred police officers were stripped of their badges and found themselves facing criminal charges in what could be described as a case of the biter bit. A hasty recruitment campaign got underway, and officers were drafted in from across the country in the interim.

The case made the House of Commons and the national news, with Dave Hunter being hailed as a people's hero by some sections of the press. This was embarrassing for the Chief Constable of Essex Police who ultimately had two choices. Either he could claim that he didn't know what was happening all this time (despite vast amounts of evidence to the contrary), or he could admit that he had suspected it but had failed to act – either was career suicide, and he knew it. Many people suspected that the mental breakdown apparently brought on by the stress of it all was a ruse to avoid answering some rather awkward questions and potentially facing prison. And they were right.

Speaking of prison, it could be said (and was by at least one red top newspaper) that Dave Hunter's blow for justice had done little to ease the problem of overcrowding. Barry Wise, Frankie Howse, Ronald Butler and Phillip Howlens were sent down for a very long time indeed, and though they spoke of revenge upon their release, they must have known that none of them was getting any younger, and therefore they were unlikely to live long enough to carry out any acts of retribution.

Slouch, by contrast, was something of a model prisoner. He didn't stand much chance of an early release – none whatsoever, in fact – but he sought a different kind of pardon entirely: he found God. This meant he spent more time with the prison chaplain than he did watching Sky Sports on the sumptuous plasma screen in the prison's large and luxurious recreation centre.

In fact, he was so reformed that he played no part in revealing the identity of several bent coppers on the inside. Others did though, and that was a business all of its own.

A great many of Norman Layer's employees also got rounded up and thrown in the hole, which was probably the best place for them now that Layer's empire had collapsed and they were out on their ears.

Dave spent some time late that summer with the sexy saxophonist who had long been the object of his affections. He suspected she felt the allure of his hero status, and he could live with that. They were taking it slowly, but Dave Hunter was a man who knew better than ever that some things were worth working at and worth waiting for. He also took small (actually great) joy from the fact that the smooth-talking Yank had not only admitted defeat and buggered off home but because he had done so thanks to him.

It was a late September afternoon with the sun low in the sky when Dave, Mick and Danny found their way to the union bar, meeting once more as they prepared for another go on the academic merry-go-round. They hadn't seen each other much since April, but that would change soon enough.

They took their usual places at a small round table away from the noisy gaming machines and the clinking pool balls and drank it all in. Nobody said anything, and nobody had to. It was the right feeling, in the right place at just the right time.

It was Freshers' Week, which explained the dozen or so young men bouncing through the SU Bar on pogo sticks dressed as Ninja Turtles.

"Best we get used to all this," said Mick.

Surprisingly, they didn't speak much of their recent adventure, the one that had brought down the largest crime syndicate since the Krays many years earlier, even though one could be forgiven for thinking they would have done. Instead, they caught up like any bunch of old mates did, albeit only briefly. For the first time in his adult life, Dave refused a second pint, although he strenuously denied this had anything to do with him being under the thumb, or that he was on his way to see her now. It did, of course, and he was, but he promised his friends they would be able to play some blues and sink a few at his house the following night, and it was a promise he would keep.

Outside, as Dave Hunter went on his way, the late, low sun's golden-yellow hue reminded him that summer would soon be out of reach. Yet his spirit didn't sink at the thought of dark nights and frosty mornings. He found himself thinking of autumn fires and wood smoke curling through October mists, and he remembered looking for conkers on the way home from school as a lad. They'll soon be burning the leaves, he thought. And that was something he looked forward to very much.

DAVE HUNTER WILL RETURN IN

MESSIN' WITH THE KID

Printed in Great Britain
by Amazon